*Hoffmann*

# RETRIBUTION

# By Mark Walden

In the H.I.V.E. series

*The Higher Institute of Villainous Education*

*The Overlord Protocol*

*Escape Velocity*

*Dreadnought*

*Rogue*

*Zero Hour*

*Aftershock*

*Deadlock*

In the Earthfall series

*Book 1: Earthfall*

# RETRIBUTION

## Book 2 of the Earthfall Trilogy

# Mark Walden

Simon & Schuster Books for Young Readers

New York   London   Toronto   Sydney   New Delhi

SIMON & SCHUSTER BOOKS FOR YOUNG READERS
An imprint of Simon & Schuster Children's Publishing Division
1230 Avenue of the Americas, New York, New York 10020

Text copyright © 2014 by Mark Walden
Jacket illustration copyright © 2015 by Mike Heath
Originally published in 2014 in Great Britain by Bloomsbury Publishing
First US edition 2015

SIMON & SCHUSTER BOOKS FOR YOUNG READERS is a trademark of Simon & Schuster, Inc.
For information about special discounts for bulk purchases, please contact Simon & Schuster Special Sales at 1-866-506-1949 or business@simonandschuster.com.
The Simon & Schuster Speakers Bureau can bring authors to your live event. For more information or to book an event, contact the Simon & Schuster Speakers Bureau at 1-866-248-3049 or visit our website at www.simonspeakers.com.
Book design by Chloë Foglia
The text for this book is set in Goudy Old Style.
Manufactured in the United States of America
0615 FFG
2 4 6 8 10 9 7 5 3 1
CIP data for this book is available from the Library of Congress.
ISBN 978-1-4424-9418-3 (hardback)
ISBN 978-1-4424-9420-6 (eBook)

*To Simon and Karen.*
*Both brilliant, but better bound.*

# RETRIBUTION

# 1

In the frozen darkness of deep space, something stirred. Pulses of energy raced through systems buried deep within a vast vessel as slowly it woke. Blood-red lights glowed on the hull of the enormous black ship as the consciousness within its heart stirred, and like a beast waking from a long hibernation the ship began to unfurl. Long, sweeping, arc-shaped pylons stretched out from the hull, lighting up in turn with a corona of crimson lightning. The entity within felt something approximating satisfaction as it received the stream of diagnostic messages. The speed and direction of the vessel was exactly as anticipated; it was less than a light-year from its target, a small blue planet orbiting an insignificant yellow star. The entity felt a moment of excitement—its long sleep was over, and soon it would be time to feed.

*　*　*

Sam woke with a start, his breath coming in ragged gasps as he sat bolt upright in bed. Another nightmare. He wondered if they would ever fade or if he would always be haunted by the faces of friends and family he had lost over the last two years. He put his hand to his forehead and just for an instant was startled by its cool metallic surface pressing against his skin. It had been a month since he had lost his hand to the Voidborn nanite swarm and he was still struggling to get used to its replacement. He turned on the small bedside light and looked down at the gleaming gold of his lower arm. He concentrated for a moment and the surface seemed to ripple as the millions of microscopic nanites that made up his limb swirled into a new configuration, the fingers of his hand turning into a smooth flat panel that reflected his face. The boy who stared back at him was very different from the slightly overweight, carefree person that he would have seen in the mirror before the Voidborn invasion.

If you could even call it that, he thought to himself.

Invasion didn't properly describe the experience of seeing an entire planet enslaved in the blink of an eye without a shot being fired. He willed his hand back into its original form, the flat panel replaced once again by slowly flexing golden fingers. He could hear the Voidborn nanites as an almost inaudible hiss in the back of his skull. It was symptomatic of the strange connection that he had with the Voidborn, something that had ultimately proved to be the decisive factor in their defeat. He still did not fully understand why it was that he had the ability to sense the alien creatures in this way—all he knew was that it gave him an edge that other survivors of the invasion seemed to lack.

"Still mostly human," Sam said to himself with a wry smile. He quickly got dressed and headed out into the snow-covered remains of St. James's Park, rubbing his hands together to warm them up before shoving them into the pockets of his camouflage-print overcoat. This winter was proving to be particularly harsh.

Sam paused for a moment and looked up at the colossal Voidborn Mothership hovering above central London. Once it had been a terrifying sight, something that had filled him with dread, but now it was strangely reassuring. The bright yellow glow of the lights that covered the enormous vessel's hull was the only indication that this Mothership was any different to the ones that were hovering above other cities all over the world. This ship was now their protector and had been ever since the mysterious nanites that swam in Sam's bloodstream had become integrated with the Voidborn consciousness that controlled it. That entity was now known as the Servant. It was something neither human nor Voidborn, but for reasons still unclear to Sam, it seemed to be on their side. The Servant could control the Mothership above them, but its connection to the rest of the Voidborn consciousness had apparently been severed completely.

"I trust you have rested well, Illuminate," the Servant said as she approached. The Servant had assumed a striking human-like appearance as a tall female with golden metallic skin and glowing yellow eyes.

"Yes, thank you," Sam replied with a nod. None of them understood what Sam's status as Illuminate actually meant, but it appeared that the Servant was programmed to protect and obey him.

"Doctor Stirling has requested that you join him in the research building," the Servant said. "He wishes to inform you of a problem that has been encountered with awakening the dormant humans."

"What kind of problem?" Sam asked with a frown.

"Doctor Stirling stated that he wishes to explain it to you personally," the Servant replied.

"Okay, tell him I'll be there in two minutes," Sam said with a quick wave to his friend Rachel, who was walking toward them.

Rachel's smile faded as she approached.

"What's up?" she asked, tucking a dangling lock of her long brown hair behind her ear.

"Not sure," Sam said, glancing toward the research building on the far side of the compound. "Stirling wants to see me—sounds like there's some kind of problem with waking the Sleepers."

"That's not good," Rachel said. "Didn't Goldie give you any more information?"

"No, she said he wants to speak to me himself. I know they've been getting close to perfecting a localized transmitter for the waking signal, but it sounds like there might have been a setback."

"Mind if I tag along?" Rachel asked.

"'Course not," Sam said. "If Stirling and Will descend into their usual technobabble, I'll need someone to keep me awake."

The two of them walked across the open central area of the compound, passing the firing range that they'd set up next to the armory. The hulking shape of a Grendel, the Voidborn's most feared soldiers, stood in front of the entrance to the armory, keeping silent, patient vigil. The creature stood thirty feet tall and was covered in black segmented bio-mechanical armor. Its low-slung head swung back and forth, its burning yellow eyes searching for any threat. Just a couple of months ago, being that close to a Grendel would have meant a very messy and unpleasant death, but now this creature and the hundreds more like it aboard the Mothership and patrolling the streets of London were their sworn protectors. It had taken some getting used to.

As the two of them approached the entrance to the research building, Dr. Iain Stirling walked outside to meet them.

"Thank you for coming at such short notice," Stirling said, rubbing his eyes. He looked as if he hadn't slept properly in a while.

"The Servant said you'd had some sort of problem with your research into waking the Sleepers," Sam said.

"Yes," Stirling replied with a sigh. "I'm afraid that the situation has become more complex than we had initially anticipated. You need to see this for yourself."

The three of them headed up to the second floor and out into a long room filled with portable army surplus cots where several dozen apparently unconscious people lay. It was a sight that Sam had witnessed many times over the past two years. This was the fate of most of humanity, enslaved instantly by an alien signal that robbed them of all free will, turning them into mindless slaves. As they had begun to explore the city more thoroughly, they had discovered hundreds of buildings that now served as huge storehouses for the enslaved millions who had once called this city their home. It was in a place not unlike this that Sam had last seen his sister, lying unconscious on the floor. That was the day the Voidborn had invaded, nearly two years ago, and it was the last time he'd seen any of his family. He and a handful of others who were immune to the effects of the signal were, as far as they knew, the last human beings on the planet with any free will.

"These places give me the creeps," Rachel said as she and Sam followed Stirling down the narrow path between the prone bodies. It led to a screened-off area at the other end of the room. "Those things floating around don't help either."

Sam glanced over at the pair of Voidborn Hunter Drones moving slowly around the room. They looked like hovering mechanical jellyfish; gleaming silver shells covered their top halves and a mass of writhing metallic tentacles hung beneath. The surface of their bodies was illuminated by fine patterns of yellow light. Once that light had been the sickly green color that was typical of Voidborn technology, but that had all changed when the Mothership above London had fallen to the human resistance.

As Sam and Rachel crossed the room, a single row of Sleepers opened their eyes and slowly climbed to their feet, their faces blank. In unison they turned and slowly walked to the other side of the room, where a large cylindrical Voidborn machine sat on a table. As the first of the Sleepers approached the machine, a hatch slid open on its front and the mute woman reached inside. There was a click and a hiss, and a few seconds later she withdrew her arm from the opening.

"Feeding time," Rachel said as the woman returned to her previous position and lay down on the cot, her eyes closed.

"They're not animals in a zoo," Stirling said, sounding irritated, as the rest of the line of silent people slid their arms into the machine one by one. "The human body requires remarkably little in the way of sustenance if it's delivered efficiently. It also dramatically reduces the amount of waste produced by the digestive system."

"Let's not go there," Sam said with a crooked smile. "There are some things that I'm happy just to leave to the Drones if that's okay with you."

The simple fact of the matter was that they still had no idea why it was that the Voidborn had taken such care to keep their human slaves in relatively good physical condition. Certainly some had been used as workers, gathering resources for the aliens or building mysterious structures, like the giant drilling rig that the resistance had disabled in St. James's Park a couple of months ago. That still didn't explain why they were so meticulous in their care of those who were either too young or too old to be of use to them.

"Through here," Stirling said, pushing aside one of the screens and ushering Sam and Rachel through the gap. In the area beyond were three beds, each containing a motionless figure. Their friend Will stood at the foot of one of the beds studying a medical chart. He glanced up and gave the others a quick nod. He looked tired.

"Any change?" Stirling asked as he joined Will, looking down at the man on the bed with a frown.

"Nothing," Will said, "but early indications are that they've fallen into comas triggered by neurological shock.

What is impossible to determine currently is how much permanent damage was caused. We could be looking at brain death. There's a very real possibility that they won't ever wake up."

"These are the ones we were trying to wake?" Rachel said quietly.

"Yes," Stirling replied with a sigh, "I'm afraid so."

"What happened to them?" Sam asked.

"As you know, the Servant and I had isolated what we believed to be the signal that could wake individuals from the Voidborn sleep," Stirling explained. "We created a portable transmitter that would allow us to broadcast the signal to a single individual and the results were . . . well . . . catastrophic. All the subjects showed clear signs of regaining consciousness and then all three suffered the same massive neurological shock. We must have missed something, some kind of fail-safe that the Voidborn have put in place to stop us from doing just this."

"And the Servant didn't know that?" Rachel asked. "She may be on our side now, but she's still Voidborn."

"The Servant has no memory of her previous existence," Stirling replied, shaking his head.

"So where does that leave us?" Sam asked. "If we can't wake up the world, how can we fight? We may have retaken the city, but there's no way we can take the fight to the Voidborn with just one Mothership. If we can't wake people up, all we can do is sit here and wait while the Voidborn do whatever they want with the rest of the planet."

"I am quite aware of that," Stirling replied, "but our understanding of Voidborn technology is still rudimentary at best and this is a perfect example of how that ignorance can have terrible consequences. It is likely that none of these three men will ever regain consciousness, but what if it had been three hundred Sleepers or three thousand? We need to proceed more carefully. These things can't be rushed. We will find an answer, it's just going to take time."

"Is there anything that we can do to help?" Rachel asked.

"Yes, actually," Stirling said. "We need an ECG monitor so that we can properly assess the brain activity in these men. As to where you would find one, your guess is as good as mine. Local hospitals, medical equipment suppliers, somewhere like that, I would imagine."

"Jay and Adam should be back from their scouting run soon," Rachel said. "Write down exactly what you need and I'll pass it on to them. If anyone can find what you need, it's those two."

"Fine, give me a couple of minutes," Stirling replied, pulling a notepad and pen from his jacket pocket before retreating to the desk in the corner of the room to put together his shopping list.

"Do you want to tell the others or shall I?" Rachel said

quietly as they walked back into the dormitory. "You know it's not going to go down well."

Sam was aware that the prospect of waking the Sleepers had been keeping the group's spirits high since the elation of the Voidborn's defeat in London. Nobody talked about it much, but they all knew it was the only way that they might ever see their friends and families again.

"I'll do it," Sam said with a sigh. "We'll get everyone together when Jay and Jack get back and tell them what Stirling told us. They may not like it, but they all need to know."

"What if Stirling's wrong, Sam?" Rachel asked as they walked down the stairs leading to the exit. "What if we never find a way to wake everyone up? How do we fight then?"

"Same way we always have," Sam replied as they stepped out into the crisp winter air. "Dirty."

"Well, that sucks," Jay said with a sigh as he collapsed back into the armchair in the living area of the team's dormitory.

"I'm going to have to agree with Jay, I'm afraid," Nat said with a nod. "So what's the plan now?"

"We can't give up," Sam replied, sitting on the edge of the table at the end of the room. "We just have to hope that Stirling and the Servant can come up with a solution."

"But there's no guarantee that they will," Adam said as he sorted the various items that he had scavenged on his last run into piles on another table. "Heads up, Jack, got something for you." He tossed a book across the room to the boy with bright red hair sitting opposite. "Don't say I never do anything for you."

"Whoa, *Anarchist's Cookbook*," Jack said with a grin as he examined the book, "a thousand ways to blow yourself up with household ingredients. Thanks, man."

"Great, remind me to thank you when we're reassembling the building," Anne said. "Jack and explosives, what could possibly go wrong?"

"So does Stirling have any idea why it didn't work?" Jay asked.

"'Fraid not," Will replied, pushing his glasses back up onto the bridge of his nose. "Just guesses at the moment, but he'll figure it out—he always does."

"Let's hope you're right," Nat said. "So what do we do in the meantime? Just sit and wait and hope that Stirling and the Servant come up with a way around the problem?"

"No," Sam said, "we can't assume that just because the Voidborn haven't attacked us and our Mothership yet that they aren't going to. We need to start planning our next move. We know from the TV coverage of the Mothership fleet's arrival that there were ships above other cities around the world, but we don't even know for sure how many were sent here to Britain. We need to know much more about the enemy's strength if we're going to take the fight to them. I know that we've all been focused on Stirling and the Servant's efforts to wake the Sleepers, but it may be that the only way to actually do that is to eliminate the Voidborn completely."

"The Servant has no ideas, I assume?" Will asked.

"No, her memory begins with the moment we first saw her on the bridge of the Mothership," Sam said, "and she has no connection to the Voidborn consciousness anymore."

"Fortunately," Adam said, "because you know that's going to be a two-way street and I don't want to be around if she ever has a change of heart about helping us."

"So we need to go look, then," Jay said. "Let's face it, another Mothership floating above Britain isn't going to be that hard to spot."

"I agree," Rachel said with a nod. "I'm tired of sitting around waiting for the Voidborn to make the next move. We've barely ventured beyond the outskirts of London since this all began. We have no idea what might be happening in the rest of the country, let alone the rest of the world."

"So how do we do this?" Anne asked. "I hear what you're saying, Jay, but, big as that thing is," she gestured upward to the ship floating unseen above them, "we can't just set off wandering randomly looking for another one.

We need some clue to where we should look."

"I believe I can help with that," Stirling said, stepping from the shadows at the other end of the room. No one had seen him come in.

"I hate it when he does that," Jay whispered to Rachel.

"I still have some printouts of telemetry data from tracking stations that were monitoring the Voidborn vessels during their final approach to Earth," Stirling continued, walking slowly toward them. "It only gives us limited local sub-orbital trajectory data, but that should be enough to let us make some educated guesses as to where some of the other Motherships went. At the very least it should help narrow the search."

"Sounds good," Sam said. "How long will it take to crunch the numbers?"

"A couple of hours," Stirling replied. "I'm afraid my orbital dynamics may be a little rusty."

"We could get the Servant to process the data," Will said. "Might be faster."

"I'm quite capable of performing the calculations myself, thank you, William," Stirling replied.

"Of course, Doctor Stirling," Will said sheepishly. "Sorry."

They had all experienced the more abrasive side of the doctor's temper at one time or another, and their recent victory over the Voidborn seemed to have done little to improve his mood.

"Once we have an approximate location we can scan more effectively for Voidborn signals and hopefully pinpoint their precise coordinates," Stirling continued. "I will discuss the necessary modifications to the Mothership's equipment with the Servant."

With that he turned and walked out of the room.

"So what are we going to do when we find out where the other Motherships are?" Jay asked Sam quietly as the others sat around chatting with one another.

"Good question," Sam said with a sigh. "It's important that we keep everyone occupied with planning this operation until Stirling and the Servant have more of an idea about what's causing the problems with the Sleepers. What we don't want right now is everyone starting to think about what it might mean if we can't ever wake them."

"Yeah, I know what you mean," Jay said, glancing over at their friends. "We've all been thinking for weeks that this was our big chance, that maybe we could wake enough people and actually strike back at the Voidborn. That's going to be a lot tougher if it's just us."

"Hey," Sam said with a smile, "*just us* managed to take control of a Voidborn Mothership. Who knows what else we could pull off if we put our minds to it."

Stirling sat at his desk in a tastefully furnished room that had once been occupied by his old colleague and traitor to humanity, Oliver Fletcher. The office was housed within the structure that the Voidborn had built around their drilling rig in St. James's Park. He studied the sheets of data, occasionally making small marks on a large map of the world that was spread out on the desk beneath them. The columns of numbers would have been meaningless to most people, but to his mind's eye they were a graceful arc plotted through the open sky.

He reached into one of his desk drawers and pulled out a ruler, using it to mark a line that passed straight through London, intersecting with the location of the one Mothership that they knew for certain, before turning to another sheet of figures and starting to make small marks on the map.

"Doctor Stirling," the Servant said as she appeared at the open door, "I am sorry to disturb you, but I have made a discovery that I believe you will find interesting."

"And what might that be?" Stirling asked without looking up from the map.

"I have been attempting a broad frequency scan as you had instructed," the Servant explained.

"And you had success?" Stirling asked.

"Not as yet," the Servant replied. "I am proceeding with caution to ensure there is no possibility that I will inadvertently re-initiate my own connection with the Voidborn."

"So what have you found then?" Stirling asked, frowning slightly as he looked up at her.

"A signal of unknown origin," the Servant replied. "Both the content and transmission frequency suggest it is human in origin."

"Human?" Stirling said, sounding surprised. "Some kind of automated beacon or distress signal probably."

"I do not believe so," the Servant replied. "I have recorded the message. Would you like me to play it back for you?"

"Yes, please do."

The Servant opened her mouth slightly wider and her own voice was replaced with a hiss of static that suddenly resolved into a man's voice.

"Hotspur two, this is Hotspur seven. We have live targets at grid seven two nine, repeat live targets. We need a Predator strike package on station now."

"Roger that Hotspur seven, Drone inbound. ETA four minutes."

Stirling's eyes widened as he listened: it was a military transmission. A moment later the signal dissolved back into white noise.

"Where did this signal come from?" Stirling demanded, all thought of sub-orbital trajectories suddenly gone from his head.

"Unfortunately, my systems were not designed for tracking such basic communication technology, which makes that more difficult to determine. Also, the transmission was very brief, making it difficult to get a precise fix on its point of origin, but it appears to have originated from somewhere in the northern region of this landmass."

"Show me," Stirling said, standing up and walking over to the large map of the British Isles that hung on the wall.

The Servant studied the map for a few seconds and then pointed at a specific location.

"My calculations suggest that this would be the nearest human population center to the point of origin for the transmission."

"Edinburgh," Stirling said. "There's someone awake in Edinburgh."

# 2

Sam walked into the meeting room with Jay. The others were already sitting on the folding metal chairs that faced the whiteboard at the other end of the room. Doctor Stirling and the Servant stood on either side of a map of the United Kingdom, waiting for them to take their seats.

"What's this all about?" Sam asked as he sat next to Rachel.

"No idea," Rachel replied. "Stirling just called for everyone to get together. He must have some sort of announcement to make."

"Do you think it's about the Sleepers?" Sam asked quietly.

"Could be," Rachel said with a shrug. "Suppose we're about to find out."

"Thank you, everyone," Stirling said, waiting a couple of seconds for everyone to quiet down. "I'm sorry to gather you all at such short notice, but there's been an exciting development." He turned to the Servant. "Please go ahead."

Stirling watched the faces of the gathered children as the Servant replayed the recording that she had shown him less than an hour earlier. Their expressions perfectly summed up his own feelings, a mixture of excitement and curiosity.

"When was this recorded?" Sam asked as the playback ended.

"The transmission occurred sixty-three minutes and fourteen seconds ago," the Servant replied.

"Do we know where it came from?" Rachel asked, gesturing to the map that stood between Stirling and the Servant.

"My calculations have narrowed the point of origin to somewhere within this area," the Servant said, picking up a marker pen and drawing a perfect circle on the map.

"That's Edinburgh," Rachel said, "but that area covers the entire city. Can't you be any more specific?"

"Not without receiving further transmissions," the Servant replied. "It was only by chance that I intercepted the first broadcast."

"And you've not heard anything else since?" Nat asked.

"No, but I am still scanning for any other transmissions," the Servant replied.

"So we got lucky," Sam said.

"Yes," Stirling replied, "so the question now is what do we do?"

"There's no guarantee that the transmission source wasn't mobile," Will said, pushing his glasses up onto the bridge of his nose. "If that's the case, intercepting more of them may not help narrow the search area—if anything it might just make it larger."

"Will's right," Anne said, nodding. "We won't necessarily get a more precise fix than we already have."

"So, the real question is, do we go take a look?" Sam said.

"Surely we have to," Nat said. "If there are other people fighting the Voidborn up there, we have to try to find them. Don't get me wrong—we're more than capable of holding our own here now that we have our own tame Mothership, but more guns on our side can't hurt, surely."

"Might not be that straightforward," Jack said, shaking his head. "What if they're not so friendly? What if they decide that they want our resources for themselves?"

"A shared foe doesn't automatically make people allies," Liz said, nodding her agreement.

"I still think we should at least go and have a look," Sam said. "We may have driven the Voidborn out of London, but we're still a long way from winning the war. Whoever these people are they sound like professional military. That's the kind of help we need."

"Yes, well, the Voidborn presence outside of London may be more relevant to this discussion than you realize," Stirling said with a slight frown.

"How so?" Rachel asked.

"My telemetry data revealed that the Voidborn Mothership heading toward the northern half of the British Isles stopped at almost exactly the same location," Stirling replied.

"So the area's probably crawling with bug-eyed creeps," Jay said.

"It will make any reconnaissance of the area more difficult," Stirling said. "I would suggest that we only send a small team. We must avoid detection until we have a better idea of what's going on up there."

"Okay," Sam said, looking at the map, "four-man team. No more. We travel light and fast, get in and out as quickly as possible. If we find whoever's giving the Voidborn a hard time up there, great. If we don't, we head back to London and think again." He turned to the Servant. "How close can a drop-ship get us without being detected by the Voidborn Mothership?" The Voidborn drop-ships were fast-moving, heavily armed aircraft that made up the bulk of their airborne forces. Their sleek, black triangular outlines were a familiar sight in the skies above London.

"If there is a Mothership in the region, as Doctor Stirling predicts, it would be unwise to bring the drop-ship within an eighteen-mile radius," the Servant replied. "Inside that range it will be impossible to conceal the energy signature of the power core from the

Voidborn sensor net, no matter how stealthy our approach."

"And they'd be able to tell we're not one of their own?" Rachel asked.

"It would be possible," the Servant replied.

"Not a chance worth taking though," Sam said. "I think Jack, Rachel, Jay, and I should go and have a discreet look around up there. We'll drop outside the city and make our way in quick and quiet."

"Hey," Nat said, "I want in too. I'm as good a shot as any of you."

"I know," Sam replied, "which is why I want you here. If something goes wrong up there we're going to need you to come and get us."

Nat looked for a moment like she was going to argue with Sam, but then she gave a reluctant nod.

"Thanks for volunteering me," Jay said. "I was just starting to get used to not having anyone shooting at me."

"I think you can handle it," Rachel replied, "or have you lost your edge over the past couple of months?"

"Least I had an edge to start with." Jay grinned.

"Okay," Sam said, "let's put together a tactical breakdown and get our kit together. We'll leave as soon as it gets dark."

Sam watched as the Voidborn drop-ship touched down in the center of the compound, its landing gear hitting the snow with a crunching thud. A hatch opened in the side of the large triangular aircraft, the patterns of yellow lights that ran in fine lines over its hull pulsing in time with the subsonic throbbing of its power core. A ramp slid down from the hatch to the ground with a soft hiss and the assembled members of the scouting team started to pick up their packs and other gear.

"Have you found us somewhere to park up there?" Sam asked the Servant.

"We have identified a suitable site."

"Good to know," Rachel said, sliding a knife into the inverted sheath on the front of her body armor and clipping it closed. "The last thing we need is a welcoming party."

"Still wish we could take a couple of these guys with us," Jay said, pointing at the Grendel patrolling the outer fence of the compound. "We might need some muscle."

"Worried you're a bit rusty, Jay?" Rachel asked with a raised eyebrow. "Been a while since you fired that thing in anger." She nodded toward the assault rifle that was leaning against his backpack a couple of yards away.

"Hey, I've logged just as many range hours as you have over the past few weeks," Jay replied indignantly. "Besides, I don't need as much practice as you do. You couldn't hit a cow's backside with a banjo."

"You two aren't going to do this for the entire flight,

are you?" Sam said with a sigh. "Because if you are I think I'll walk."

Jack jogged toward them from the direction of the armory carrying a large black hard case.

"Sorry I'm late, guys," he said, catching his breath. "Just had to go grab my new toy."

"Is that the gun that you found at the Woolwich Arsenal?" Sam asked as Jack placed the case on the ground, popping open the clips and lifting the lid.

Jack sighed. "This isn't *a* gun, it's *the* gun. The Barrett M107 sniper rifle, the perfect way to finish an argument."

"That's what I call a bullet," Jay said with a low whistle as he reached down and took one of the six-inch-long rounds from the ammunition compartment of the case.

"Big enough to punch through Grendel armor, I reckon," Jack replied. "Only one real way to find out, I suppose."

"Well, you're not testing it on Tiny," Rachel said, nodding toward the patrolling behemoth that guarded the compound.

"You named the Grendel?" Jay said.

"Yup," Rachel said, "you should be grateful I didn't go with Anne's suggestion."

"Dare I ask?" Sam said.

"Friendel," Rachel replied.

"Okay, your name's better," Jack said, "though I'd

rather not go toe to toe with any of his brothers in Scotland if we can possibly avoid it."

They had become quite used to the fact that the Voidborn in London were no longer hostile. The thought of having to go up against a Grendel that was out for their blood left a cold knot in Jack's stomach.

"Okay, let's mount up," Sam said, trying to ignore the nervousness he was starting to feel. "We've got a hike at the other end of this trip and I don't want to get caught in daylight by a Voidborn patrol."

The other three members of the scouting party slung their packs and weapons over their shoulders and walked quickly up the ramp and into the comparative warmth of the drop-ship's passenger compartment. As they walked into the black-walled space, four smooth, sculpted seats slid out from the walls.

"Goldie finally got around to giving us somewhere to sit in these things,' Rachel said, stowing her gear at the rear of the compartment before sitting down. "Nice."

"I am glad that you approve of my changes," the Servant said. Her familiar, slightly digital-sounding voice seemed to come from the walls around them.

"Maybe some cushions next time?" Jay asked.

"It's fine, thank you," Sam said, elbowing Jay in the ribs as he took his seat. "We should get going."

"Understood," the Servant replied. A moment later the fine patterns of yellow light in the black glass floor began to pulse faster and the low-pitched hum of the drop-ship's power core increased in volume as the ship lifted straight up from the ground. There were no windows to give the passengers any sense of their surroundings, but the lurch in his stomach was enough to tell Sam that they were climbing fast. Just a few seconds later he felt the direction of travel change as the drop-ship switched to forward thrust, sending them rocketing toward their destination.

"Flight time will be approximately twenty-five minutes," the Servant reported.

"Let me get something straight," Jay whispered to Sam as Rachel and Jack checked their kit. "This drop-ship is part of the Mothership right? And the Mothership *is* the Servant, so all Voidborn tech in London is part of her, yeah?"

"Pretty much," Sam replied with a nod. "So?"

"So we're pretty much sitting inside her right now," Jay said. "Which is weird."

"I'd have thought you'd be used to weird by now," Sam said, shaking his head with a chuckle.

The rest of the flight passed without incident, giving all of them one last opportunity to check their gear. None of them really knew what they might be flying into, so they had equipped themselves for as many different eventualities as possible. Sam checked his weapon, removing and reinserting the magazine and checking his safety was engaged. Reassuring as their weapons were, he hoped very much that the four of them would find the source of the mysterious transmission without ever having to use them. It was always best to avoid a noisy, attention-grabbing gunfight, especially if Stirling was right about there being a Voidborn Mothership nearby.

"We are approaching the landing site," the Servant reported. "Touchdown in fifteen seconds. Extinguishing interior illumination."

Sam felt the same shift in gravity as the drop-ship began its descent and the cabin was plunged into darkness. Just a few seconds later they landed with a soft thud. Sam snapped his night-vision goggles down into place and the passenger compartment was suddenly visible again, illuminated in a lurid green. The hatch hissed open and the four scouts quickly jogged down the ramp, spreading out across the field that the Servant had selected as their landing site. Sam dropped to one knee once he was twenty yards from the drop-ship, raising his weapon and scanning the silent snow-covered field for any sign of the Voidborn. The other three scouts followed suit, each checking their own quadrant of the surrounding countryside for any potential threat.

"Clear," Rachel reported, her voice crackling over his earpiece.

"Ditto," Jay said, "I got nothing."

"Clear here too," Jack said.

"Okay," Sam said quietly into his throat mic. "Looks like we've avoided a welcoming party. Pull back another thirty miles, but stay on station. No telling when we might need a fast pick-up."

"Understood," the Servant replied.

A moment later the alien drop-ship rose silently into the starry sky before accelerating away into the distance.

"Let's just hope that our arrival went unnoticed," Rachel said as the four of them crossed the field, heading for the country lane on the far side, their boots crunching through the undisturbed snow.

"I guess we'll find out soon enough if it didn't," Jay said, opening the gate leading to the road. "Keep your eyes open, guys. We have no idea what we're walking into here."

Over the next couple of hours they picked their way through the deserted outskirts of Edinburgh, the snow-covered fields giving way to long-abandoned suburbs. It quickly became clear that the Voidborn Mothership that they had expected to find hovering above the city was nowhere to be seen. Sam couldn't help but feel slightly relieved, even if it did now present them with the equally troubling question of where it actually was, if not here.

"So where the hell are the Voidborn?" Jack asked as they walked through the deserted back streets, heading for the center of the city. "Stirling seemed pretty sure that this was where we'd find them."

"No idea," Rachel said, pushing her night-vision goggles up onto her forehead and squinting into the gloom. "We need to find somewhere to hole up for the day. Just because we haven't found any Voidborn yet doesn't mean they're not here and, if they are, I don't want to get caught out in the open in daylight."

"Agreed," Sam said, checking his watch. The first light of dawn was appearing on the horizon. "Let's find a good hideout and keep watch for a few hours. If there's still no sign of Voidborn activity, we can concentrate on trying to find any trace of whoever made that transmission."

"That looks good," Jack said, pointing to a hotel, one of the tallest buildings nearby. "We could set up a nice discreet little observation post on the top floor and keep an eye out for any visitors."

The others nodded their agreement and hurried over to the entrance of the building. The once grand marble floor of the lobby was now half covered in snow. Suitcases and bags lay on the floor where their enslaved owners had mindlessly abandoned them nearly two years ago. Jay pointed to a door on the other side of the lobby marked "Stairs."

"You guys head up and check out the upper floors," Jay said. "I'll keep watch on the street."

Rachel nodded, gesturing for Sam and Jack to cover her. She opened the door and stepped into the stairwell beyond, weapon raised, scanning for any sign of a

"Because I mean there is *literally* nothing out there," Jay said, looking back toward the street outside. "No birds, no dogs, nothing. You know what it's like in London with the strays."

Sam knew exactly what he meant; one of the consequences of the Voidborn attack had been huge numbers of abandoned pet dogs that soon formed large feral packs, a phenomenon that was just one of the reasons that they all still carried weapons when on patrol in London.

"Could just be the weather," Sam said as the snowfall began to intensify outside. "They're probably taking shelter somewhere and waiting for it to pass."

"I suppose," Jay said, "but I can't shake the feeling that something about this just seems off. Gives me the creeps."

"Well, we'll check the center of town later and see what we can find," Sam said. "If it's as dead there as it is here, we'll head back to the pick-up point. Maybe Stirling and the Servant will have a better idea of where we should be looking by then. In the meantime, go and try to get a couple of hours' sleep. We'll head in as soon as it gets dark."

"Okay, keep your eyes peeled," Jay said with a nod, picking up his pack and slinging his rifle over his shoulder. "You see anything you call, okay?"

"Yes, Mother," Sam replied.

"Hey, if my mom was here, the Voidborn would be the least of your worries," Jay replied with a crooked smile.

Sam watched as Jay crossed the lobby, before turning his attention back to the street outside. After he had been watching for nearly half an hour, he started to feel some of the prickling unease that Jay had been talking about. The street outside was as quiet as the grave, a feeling enhanced by the gently falling snow that covered everything in its sound-deadening blanket. There was also this vague whisper at the back of his skull. It was nothing like the strange sensation that he felt when his implant reacted to the presence of the Voidborn—this was different, more like a nagging sense that there was something they'd missed.

Sam shivered. The temperature in the lobby couldn't have been much above freezing and the wind was beginning to blow in through the front doors, bringing with it flurries of fresh snow. He huddled up inside his heavy coat and tried to focus on what they still had to do. The vague sense of excitement that he had felt earlier at finally being back in action had gone, replaced by a feeling that he had not wanted to experience ever again. The feeling that they were being hunted.

Sam heard the familiar high-pitched whine as his night-vision goggles activated, illuminating the darkened street outside the hotel in shades of green. They had watched and waited all day, but there had been no sign of life, human or otherwise.

"Okay, let's go," Sam said, heading out of the door and into the street. The wind had dropped but the fresh snowfall had already blown into thick drifts that concealed all sorts of obstacles, and at times the four of them were slowed to a crawl. As they made their way closer to the center, the buildings around them grew taller, their looming shapes making the ice-bound streets feel almost like valleys in some high mountain range.

A few minutes later Rachel held a clenched fist aloft and the others quickly spread out across the street, taking up cover positions as she pulled a map from her coat pocket.

"Okay, we're at the west end of Princes Street," Rachel said as she looked up from the map at the surrounding buildings. "There's no mistaking that thing." In the distance, just visible atop its ancient volcanic crag, outlined against the night sky, was the imposing shape of Edinburgh Castle.

"There's nothing here, man," Jay said, shaking his head.

"Even if there was, we'd never find it buried under all this snow," Jack said with a sigh.

"We've got a few more hours before we need to head back to the pick-up point," Sam said. "Let's take advantage of the time we've got and make sure that we don't miss anything. If there are other people awake here, we have to try to find them. At least we haven't run into any Voidborn yet."

"Starting to wish that we would," Jay said, scanning their surroundings. "Never thought I'd say that."

"Let's work our way up to the castle and then head back out of the center," Sam said. "We need to be out of here before it starts to get light."

The others fell into line behind him as he walked slowly down the broad road that had once been the busiest street in the city. The abandoned cars were barely visible beneath the snow drifts. The tattered shopfronts looked like cave entrances, their frozen interiors hidden in blackness that even night-vision systems struggled to penetrate. The wind was starting to pick up again and what had once been a persistent but gentle snowfall rapidly transformed into swirling eddies of ice that stung any exposed skin they found. Sam flexed the fingers of his left hand, trying to convince his numb fingers that they wanted to maintain their grip on his rifle. His other, less human hand felt perfectly warm, but then he supposed that now it always would, whatever the conditions.

Sam was peering into the increasingly dense cloud of snow that lay ahead of them, when a hideous, unearthly howl came from nearby. It was like nothing he had ever heard before, somewhere between agony and terror, and it made his gut tense in pure, instinctive fear.

"What the hell was that?" Rachel whispered as the four of them sought cover behind the snow-covered vehicles.

"Nothing good," Jay said, his head snapping from side to side as he strained to spot any sign of movement in the rapidly developing blizzard. Another screeching howl came from a different direction, off to their right, and then was answered in turn by another somewhere behind them. The hairs on the back of Sam's neck prickled as he felt a sudden, almost primal fear.

"We should pull back," Rachel said. "Whatever that is, we can't fight in these conditions. We need more cover."

"Agreed," Sam said with a quick nod.

"What about in there?" Jay said quickly, jerking his head toward the front of a department store.

Sam quickly weighed their options. It would be dark in there and they ran the risk of getting trapped, but they had their night-vision goggles and they were far too exposed out here on the street. From somewhere off in the darkness there was another shrieking howl and Sam quickly made a decision.

"Okay," he barked, "everyone inside. We find a good spot and let whatever's out there come to us."

The four of them dashed across the street and inside the gloomy store. They were surrounded by displays for cosmetics and perfumes, all now covered in a fine layer of snow, relics of a lifestyle that seemed like very distant history. They ran past the gaudy displays, weapons raised, heading deeper inside, constantly scanning for any sign of movement or threat.

"Head upstairs," Sam said, pointing over toward the escalators in the middle of the ground floor.

"You sure?" Rachel asked, glancing over her shoulder anxiously as more unearthly howls came from outside. Whatever it was that was out there was certainly no pack of feral dogs. "We could get trapped up there."

"If there are enough Voidborn outside, we could get trapped anywhere," Sam replied. "We need to find a good firing position, somewhere we can hold out until this storm passes."

"Sam's right," Jay said with a nod as they approached the escalators. "We don't stand a chance out there. We need to hunker down."

"Well, let's find some cover fast," Jack said, swallowing nervously. "Because whatever it is, it's getting closer."

The four of them sprinted up the metal staircase, taking the steps two at a time. The next floor was filled with dust-covered racks of clothes and the slightly creepy humanoid silhouettes of mannequins frozen in mid-pose. They ran between the displays, hunting for a place to take cover.

"There," Sam snapped, pointing at the far end of the floor where they could just make out the tables and chairs of a café. Sam led the others through the dining area, leaping over the stainless-steel counter and pushing the swing doors that led to the kitchen open just a crack, enough so that he could see what was on the other side. He surveyed the empty kitchen quickly and then turned back to the others.

"Okay, we set up here," he said, gesturing back toward the escalators. "If anything comes up, we should have no problem spotting them. If it looks like we're going to get overrun, then fall back to the kitchen. There's plenty of cover, and stairs on the other side that give us an escape route if we need it."

"Stairs work both ways you know," Jack said with a frown as he unfolded the bi-pod from beneath the barrel of his sniper rifle before resting it on top of one of the display cases filled with the gray, desiccated remains of the snacks that the café used to serve. "We don't want to get trapped in here."

"I know," Sam said. "I'll watch our backs—just get ready to fight."

Sam fought to keep the nervousness from his voice. He had no idea what was out there, but he did know one thing: it was nothing they'd seen before. If they were going to get out in one piece, they were going to need to keep their heads clear. From somewhere below them they heard a muffled crash, and Sam felt the hairs on the back of his neck stand up. It had only been a few months since they had last fought the Voidborn, but that didn't stop the slight tremor in his human hand caused by the sudden rush of adrenaline that was surging through his system.

"Okay," Sam whispered as the others took cover behind the counter, their weapons trained on the escalators fifty yards away. "Don't open fire unless you have to. I'd much rather avoid a fight here if we possibly can. We still don't know where the main Voidborn forces are, but you can bet that a pitched gun battle is going to bring them running."

"Gotcha," Jay said as Rachel gave a quick nod.

Sam peered out into the darkness, the limited range of his night-vision goggles turning the gloomy shop floor into a confusing jumble of indistinct shadowy objects.

"You see anything?" Jay whispered to Jack as he slowly swung the massive sniper rifle left and right, using the thermal-imaging system built into its scope to scan for targets.

"Nope," Jack replied quietly, "but it's gone awfully quiet all of a sudden."

The howling had stopped. Whatever was downstairs was now moving in silence, hunting them. Sam clicked the safety off on his rifle, his finger slipping inside the guard and curling around the trigger.

"Movement," Jack whispered as he saw something flicker through his sights. Whatever it was, its heat signature was barely visible, nothing like the rainbow hues of a normal person's thermal image. "Definitely not human."

Sam sighted down the barrel of his rifle, waiting for a

clear shot. There was a flash of movement around the escalators and he had a fleeting glimpse of a humanoid form.

"You sure about that?" he whispered to Jack. "Looked pretty human to me."

"The only people with heat signatures like that are dead people," Jack said.

There was a thunderous double bang as Rachel opened fire at something.

"Definitely humanoid," Rachel said, "too fast to be human, though."

She had only glimpsed the figure for a second, just enough time for a pot shot, but whatever she'd fired at had vanished, her bullets passing through empty air.

"What the hell is th—"

Sam never finished his question as dozens of figures burst from hiding amidst the displays surrounding the escalators and began sprinting at impossible speed toward them. The creatures might once have been human, but now they looked like something from the deepest recesses of a nightmare.

Their swollen, misshapen skulls were elongated and swept back with tiny blackened eyes on either side of noses that were little more than two oozing slits in the center of their faces. Their mouths were lined with two-inch-long crystalline teeth, their jaws opening impossibly wide as they howled in unison, signaling their attack.

Their naked bodies were covered in black veins that bulged horribly as the creatures sprinted toward them, the long glinting talons at the tips of their spindly fingers outstretched.

Sam felt a fleeting moment of hesitation as his horrified mind tried to make sense of what he was seeing. If these things had ever been human, they had been corrupted beyond recognition.

"Take them!" Jay yelled, firing a short burst into the lead creature. The bullets hit the creature in the chest, knocking it spinning off its feet, its twitching body sliding to a halt, its companions not even slowing as they raced past their fallen pack mate.

The four of them opened fire, the constant roar of Sam, Jay, and Rachel's weapons punctuated by the massive booms from Jack's sniper rifle.

"On your left," Jay yelled at Jack as he saw a flicker of movement in the periphery of his vision. Jack swiveled the rifle on its mount and fired, the massive bullet striking a hole the size of a grapefruit clean through the creature. It fell beside another of its companions, which lay twitching in a pool of black blood.

"Keep firing!" Sam shouted as more of the creatures poured toward them from the escalators, barely slowed by the mounting bodies of their fallen.

"You've got to be kidding me," Jay said, as he saw the first one of the creatures that he had hit slowly pushing itself back to its feet, despite the massive injuries it had suffered.

"We're going to be overrun," Sam cried out. "Everyone fall back!"

Jack slung the sniper rifle over his shoulder and pulled the pistol from the holster on his hip, shooting into the mass of monsters while slowly backing toward the door leading to the kitchen. The others followed suit, firing at the swarm of creatures as they retreated, trying desperately to stem the nightmarish tide.

"What are these things?" Rachel spat through gritted teeth as she fired another burst.

"I don't know," Sam said, pushing the kitchen door open and glancing inside, "and I'm not sure I want to. Looks clear, let's go."

They all hurried through the door, Jay firing one last burst before slamming it shut.

"Here, give me a hand," Sam said, pushing hard on a large steel cabinet that stood to one side of the door. Jay joined in and they sent the heavy unit slamming down on to the floor, blocking the entrance with a crash. Moments later something heavy rammed against the door, shaking the frame.

"That's not going to hold them for long," Sam said. "We have to get out of here."

"We can't go back outside," Jack said, sounding slightly panicked. "We have no idea how many more of those things are out there."

There was a sound of splintering wood as the barricaded door began to give way.

"We head for the roof," Sam said. "From there we can signal the drop-ship for a pick-up. At full throttle it shouldn't be more than a couple of minutes away."

"I thought it was too risky to bring the drop-ship into the city," Rachel said as they hurried across the darkened kitchen to the door marked "Fire Exit" on the far wall.

"That was when we thought that there was a Mothership here," Sam said, taking up position on one side of the door. "Besides, we either risk it or get torn to pieces by those things. Your call."

"You're getting no argument from me," Jay said, moving to the other side of the exit. "You ready?"

Sam gave a quick nod and Jay slammed the door open, weapon raised, covering the stairs leading upward. Sam followed right behind him, scanning the stairwell below for any sign of movement.

"Clear," Jay yelled, heading up the stairs.

"Clear," Sam responded as Jack and Rachel followed them into the stairwell.

Behind them was a splintering crash followed by the sound of scraping metal on the tiled floor as the things that were pursuing them forced their way past the hastily improvised barricade. The four of them bolted up the stairs, heading for the roof, knowing that their pursuers would only be seconds behind. Sam took up the rear, trying to resist the urge to look back over his shoulder as he took the stairs three at a time. He didn't need to look— the growling sounds of ravenous pursuit from below them were more than enough to keep him moving.

Jay was the first to reach the top of the stairs, slamming his shoulder against the door leading to the roof. It didn't budge.

"Locked," Jay said, leveling his rifle at the door's handle.

"Whoa," Rachel yelled, pushing Jay's rifle barrel down toward the floor. "That's a solid steel door. You start shooting it up there's going to be bullets flying everywhere in here. Jack, you're up."

Jack gave a quick nod and unslung his pack from his back before reaching inside.

"I'm gonna need a minute," he said breathlessly.

Sam nodded and unclipped one of the anti-personnel grenades from his combat harness. The others pulled back from the stairs, flattening themselves against the wall. Sam wrenched the pin from the grenade and released the striker lever, taking a breath and making a silent count of two in his head before dropping it over the edge. The grenade fell through space as Sam turned his back to the stairs, his fingers going to his ears. A split second later there was an impossibly bright flash from below followed by a thunderous boom, the concussion wave almost knocking Sam off his feet. For a moment, he could hear only the ringing in his ears as clouds of smoke began to billow up from below, but then, as his hearing returned, he could hear the screeching howls of the injured creatures that had been caught in the blast. Sam peered over the edge and could make out nothing through the clouds of smoke other than the flickering light of a fire. There were still sounds of movement down there and Sam realized that all he had really done was buy them some time.

"Jack," Sam said, "I need that door open."

"Ten seconds," Jack said, trying to ignore the smoke irritating his lungs. "I mess this up and you'll know all about it."

He placed the cube of plastic explosive on the door's locking mechanism and then inserted a small pencil-shaped device.

"Fire in the hole," he yelled, turning away from the door as the charge detonated, destroying the lock mechanism with a bang. Jack gave the smoking door a quick, hard kick and snow blew in from the darkness outside.

"Let's go!" Sam yelled as he began to see dark shapes moving in the smoke just a couple of floors below. The others did not need to be told twice, sprinting out onto the store's windswept roof. Sam reached into one of the pockets on his belt and pulled out the small black crystal that would act as an emergency beacon to the drop-ship. He felt the Voidborn technology inside the crystal responding to him and with a small mental nudge he gave it a silent instruction to transmit. It might be risky, but there was no way they were getting out of there without it. Sam heard another series of howls from the stairwell and unclipped the second and final grenade from his harness. He tossed the grenade through the door and then ran over toward the others as it detonated behind him with a satisfying thump.

"Cover the door," Sam yelled over the howling wind. "The drop-ship should be on its way."

The four of them raised their weapons, training them on the doorway, which now had smoke pouring from it. Barely ten seconds later the first of the creatures burst out of the smoke, galloping on all fours across the roof toward them, its razor-lined mouth wide open. All four of them opened fire and the creature was cut down, falling in a twitching heap just a few yards from their feet. More of them began to pour out of the door, almost climbing over each other in their eagerness to reach their prey. The sound of gunfire became constant as the four members of the scouting party slowly retreated, firing all the time as they backed toward the edge of the roof. Sam looked over his shoulder as he felt his heel hit the low parapet that ran around the edge of the roof. It was a nine-story drop straight down to the pavement.

"Reloading!" Jay yelled, the empty clip falling from his rifle and clattering to the ground as he slammed another into place. The creatures were dropping like flies under the hail of gunfire, but their numbers did not appear to be diminishing in the slightest. They were advancing relentlessly and their prey had nowhere left to run.

"I'm out!" Rachel yelled, dropping her rifle and unholstering her pistol in one fluid movement. She fired twice and then glanced over at Sam, her expression matching the feeling in Sam's gut perfectly.

They weren't going to make it.

Sam glanced back over the edge of the roof as the creatures closed in on them. It was a long way down, but better that than being eaten alive. Suddenly, he was almost knocked off his feet as the down draft from the drop-ship's engines hit him, the soft yellow lights on its hull appearing without warning from the swirling clouds of snow. The hatch in its side slid open, level with the roof, a three-feet-wide gap between the snow-covered concrete and the safety within.

"GO!" Sam bellowed, turning back toward the advancing creatures who now scrambled to climb over the piled-up bodies of their fallen, as if suddenly realizing that their prey might escape. He fired a couple of bursts into the nearest of the monsters as Jack leaped across the gap and into the safety of the waiting drop-ship.

"Ladies first," Jay called to Rachel, and she shot him an icy glare before running toward the hovering vessel and leaping inside.

"You're next," Sam urged. "I'm right behind you."

Jay gave a quick nod and then followed the other two, jumping onboard the drop-ship and turning to offer his hand to Sam.

"Come on!" Jay shouted. "We're leaving!"

Sam felled one more of the creatures and then sprinted for the drop-ship. He sprang across the gap and caught Jay's outstretched hand just as one of the pursuing creatures reached the edge of the roof and leaped behind him. The monster's outstretched claws caught Sam's ankle in a vice-like grip, and the creature dangled below the drop-ship as it drifted away from the roof. Sam's hand slipped from Jay's and he flailed for a handhold. His fingers brushed past the edge of the door and for one fleeting instant he was framed in the doorway, a look of horror on his face before silently toppling backward into the snow-filled void.

"SAM, NO!" Jay yelled, desperately flinging himself after his friend. Rachel, grabbing the back of his combat harness, stopped him from also falling to his doom.

"Take us down," Jack yelled at the air.

"That is impossible," the Servant replied, her voice coming from all around them. "The area below is too hostile to attempt a landing."

"What do you mean?" Rachel demanded. "Take us down now!"

"I am sorry—I cannot," the Servant replied. One of the drop-ship's bulkheads shimmered for an instant and then resolved into a thermal image of the area below them. The entire street was filled with countless thousands of the creatures they had just been fighting, their faint heat signatures blurring together into one seething mass.

"Oh my God," Rachel said, her voice a broken whisper. Behind her Jay stifled a sob. Their friend was nowhere to be seen. Not even the fading heat of his body was visible. Sam was gone.

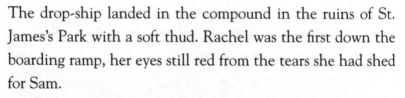

3

The drop-ship landed in the compound in the ruins of St. James's Park with a soft thud. Rachel was the first down the boarding ramp, her eyes still red from the tears she had shed for Sam.

"Rachel, what's wrong?" Nat asked.

"It's . . . it's Sam," Rachel said, her voice cracking. "He didn't make it."

Nat's mouth fell open in shock as Jay and Jack slowly walked down the ramp, looks of grief-stricken shock on their faces too. "Oh God, no," she whispered, feeling her stomach lurch. "What happened?"

"It was . . . There was . . . It was horrible," Rachel said, fresh tears trickling down her cheeks. "He never stood a chance."

Doctor Stirling approached, looking older and more tired than any of them could remember. "I'm so very sorry," he said. "The Servant informed me of the situation. Sam was a very brave young man. I'm sure we will all miss him, but we need to debrief immediately."

"Seriously?" Rachel said angrily, jabbing her finger into his chest. "Is that it? Sam's dead, the person who saved all our lives, the person who let us take London back from the Voidborn, and that's all you've got to say? Well, screw your bloody debriefing. I have a friend to grieve for."

"I know how much this hurts," Stirling said to Rachel's back as she stormed away, "but we have to understand what these creatures are. They're like nothing we've ever seen before—this could be a whole new threat."

"Leave it, Doc," Jay said quietly.

"But you don't understand," Stirling said, "if this is some new sort of Voidborn weapon, we need to understand more about it so that we can properly defend our—"

"I said *leave it*," Jay hissed.

Stirling opened his mouth as if to say something else, but the expression on Jay's face made him think twice. He watched in silence as the other young men and women who might just represent mankind's last hope for concerted resistance to the Voidborn slowly gathered around Jay and Jack, their shared grief obvious.

In the dormitory, Rachel sat down on her bed and buried her head in her hands, trying desperately to forget the last image of Sam that she had burned into her memory, the single look of fleeting horror on his face before he was gone forever. She wiped the tears from her cheeks with the back of her hand just as there was a soft knock at the door.

"Go away," Rachel said, her voice hoarse. "Whatever it is, I'm not interested."

"As you wish," the Servant replied. "I have something important to discuss with you, but we may address the situation later if you prefer."

Rachel took a deep breath before standing up and opening the door. The Servant was walking away down the corridor.

"Wait," Rachel said. "What do you want?"

The Servant turned and looked at Rachel with something that almost seemed like curiosity.

"I have been given certain instructions that I must follow in the event of the death of the Illuminate," the Servant replied.

"Sam," Rachel said quietly, "his name is . . . was . . . Sam."

"The Illuminate made his wishes quite clear as to what should happen if he were killed. I am to answer only to his chosen successor."

"Okay, so now you belong to Stirling. What's that got to do with me?" Rachel said impatiently.

"I fear you misunderstand me," the Servant replied. "Doctor Stirling was not the Illuminate's chosen successor. You were."

"Me?" Rachel asked, sounding bewildered. "Why? I

don't have any connection with the Voidborn other than this damn chip Stirling put in my head when I was a baby. I'm not like Sam—I don't have some kind of weird psychic bond with you or the Mothership. I can't control the Voidborn or anything like that, so what exactly is it that makes me qualified to take over from him?"

"You were chosen by the Illuminate—it is not my place to question his decisions. My only function now is to serve your will."

"Just what I need," Rachel said with a sigh, "something else to worry about. Stirling's going to love this."

"Is there anything I can do to assist?" the Servant asked.

"No, not really," Rachel said, shaking her head. "Just help Stirling work out what those things in Edinburgh were. We need to find some way to stop them, because I have a horrible feeling that this won't be the last we see of them."

"Understood," the Servant replied. "I will render whatever assistance Doctor Stirling requires."

The gold-skinned machine turned to walk away.

"Did you feel it?" Rachel asked. "When Sam died."

"No," the Servant replied, turning back toward her, "that was not the nature of the connection between us. I could sense his presence when he interfaced with a part of my consciousness in some way, but that was all. The Illuminate is gone; you are his successor. I do not *feel* anything. That would be an emotional response and as such it is not possible for me to experience it."

"So you don't care," Rachel said, feeling her usual resentment toward the Servant's cold, mechanical nature.

"I cannot care," the Servant replied. "It is not part of my architecture."

"Yeah? Well, sometimes I envy you," Rachel said, feeling the knot of grief in her gut. "I really do."

*Everything hurts*, Sam thought to himself. *Everything really, really hurts, but that's a good sign. It means I'm not dead.*

*First question*, he thought. *Why am I not dead?*

He slowly opened his eyes and looked around. He was in a long, narrow chamber, but it was hard to make out any detail as only the faintest gray light filled the space. A slightly brighter light was coming from somewhere above and behind him, but he couldn't crane his neck to make out exactly where because it would involve moving, and right now his entire body was telling him that trying to move would be a massive mistake.

*So you're just going to lie here and freeze to death, then?* Sam thought to himself. *Great plan.*

He took a deep breath and tried to push himself up off the floor. The sudden searing pain in his side made him feel slightly light-headed and he fought the overwhelming urge just to lie back down again, but he knew that would only end one way . . . not well. He gingerly touched his side and his fingers came away wet with blood. He took a breath and forced himself to feel the wound area again, his fingertips brushing against something cold, hard and sharp that was protruding from under the edge of the body armor beneath his armpit.

"Whatever it is, don't pull it out," Sam said to himself, trying to remember his field-medic training. Pain was better than bleeding to death—that much he knew. He sat there for a moment or two, building up his strength for the next challenge: standing up. He made it to one knee before the pain in his side and back made him stop to catch his breath. As his eyes began to adjust to the gloom, he slowly realized where he was. The long, narrow chamber was lined with snow-covered windows that were only letting in the barest splash of light, but he could just make out the shape of the seats that surrounded him. As he began to see more detail, he realized that those seats were separated by a central aisle that led down to another single seat with a steering wheel in front of it.

"How the hell did I end up on a bus?" Sam said, slowly standing up. He turned around and saw the source of the brighter overhead illumination: the soft dawn light outside poured through the shattered remains of the large skylight in the bus roof. On the roof outside he could see snow piled nearly three feet deep. His last memory was of losing his grip on Jay and then falling into blackness. He must have hit the snow, and that and his pack absorbed the brunt of the impact. Their combined weight had presumably proven too much for the skylight, which had given way beneath him, dumping him inside. He supposed that made him incredibly lucky, but he certainly didn't feel it at that precise moment.

He carefully unslung his pack from his back, ignoring the pain in his side, and assessed the damaged contents. He had enough rations for a couple of days and a rudimentary first-aid kit, but, besides a simple bivouac kit, that was pretty much all that had survived the fall. His radio was smashed to pieces and his rifle was nowhere to be seen. He felt for the holster at his waist and was relieved to touch the reassuringly cold metal of the handgun that was still clipped inside it. It was quiet outside, but that didn't mean he was alone. The hideous creatures that had chased them up onto the roof could still be anywhere, and so he was very relieved to find himself not completely unarmed. He gathered up the remnants of his pack before moving quietly toward the front of the bus. The dawn light was growing brighter, but the snow that covered the windows made it impossible to see anything. He thumped the windshield a couple of times, trying to dislodge some of the snow, but it was firmly frozen in place.

"Well, I can't stay here," Sam said to himself. He looked around for a second before spotting the emergency manual-release lever above the bus's folding doors. He pulled it, and there was a clunk from inside the wall.

Sam slid his fingers between the black rubber seals in the center of the door and pulled. The pain that shot up his side was excruciating, making him feel faint for a second, but he had to get the doors open. He took a deep breath and pulled again, but it was no good. The doors wouldn't budge. It was either the weight of snow piled up against them or else the long-neglected locking mechanism had simply jammed. He needed something to lever the doors open, but a quick inspection of the abandoned bags around the bus revealed no suitable tools. He looked up at the shattered skylight, but there was no way he was climbing back up through there with the injury in his side. There was only one option. He walked to the front of the bus and pulled the pistol from his holster, leveling it at the windshield. The sound of the shot was bound to attract attention, but that was a chance he would have to take. He wasn't going to starve to death trapped inside this thing. His finger tensed on the trigger.

"You idiot," Sam said to himself, releasing the pressure on the trigger and lowering his gun. He slid the pistol back into its holster and then pulled the black leather glove off his right hand. The golden skin beneath gleamed in the pale morning light. Sam concentrated for a second and his hand slowly reformed, morphing into a long rod with a sharpened end. He slid the newly formed tool between the doors and used it to lever them apart with a groan of corroded gears. He concentrated again and the bar reformed into the shape of an axe, which Sam swung into the frozen snow beyond the doors, carving himself an exit while ignoring the protesting jolts of pain from his side.

A few minutes later he broke through and pale sunlight streamed into the bus's interior. He continued to hack at the snow until he'd made a hole big enough to squeeze through. He took a breath and willed his hand back into its original shape, the liquid metal flowing and reforming into fingers and a thumb. He pulled the glove back over his metallic hand and took the pistol from his holster once more before squeezing through the gap and out into the daylight.

The street outside was quiet. The only sign that remained of the hideous creatures from the previous night were hundreds of hand and footprints in the snow. Sam tried to take in the sheer number of tracks that surrounded him, but it was obvious even to the untrained eye that there had been hundreds, maybe thousands of the creatures outside when he fell. He realized that he and his friends had had no idea what they were walking into, and that lack of information had very nearly cost them their lives.

"Still might, kiddo," he said to himself quietly, looking down the broad snow-covered road ahead of him. He had to find shelter before the creatures came back. He didn't relish the thought of a second encounter with them.

As he walked down Prince's Street, he considered his options. He had to find some way of communicating with the others—that much was obvious. The fact that they weren't already there looking for him told him that they must have made the not unreasonable assumption that he was dead. The only way he was going to be able to tell them otherwise was if he somehow managed to get his hands on a radio, and that meant finding the source of the mysterious transmission that they had come here to investigate in the first place.

Sam walked on, alert to the slightest sound, but the city was as quiet as a grave. He hoped that might mean that the creatures were nocturnal, but he knew that was a dangerous assumption. Regardless, he was not going to be out on the street come nightfall—that much he did know. He had maybe seven or eight hours before it got dark and before that he needed to get a better view of the city. He looked up at the castle perched on top of its massive plug of volcanic rock and decided that was his next stop. It would afford him a good view of the center of the city and would also give him somewhere to hole up for the night if necessary.

He continued down the street, the blanket of snow covering the abandoned relics of humanity's previous existence. In some ways that was better than having to see the signs of his former life, but it also gave him the acute sense that there was a great deal hidden just below the surface of the city. Whatever the creatures were that had attacked them the previous night, they were like nothing the Voidborn had thrown at them before. He tried not to dwell on their humanoid appearance; if they had indeed once been people, no shred of their humanity now remained.

Sam turned off the broad thoroughfare and down a street that led past the railway station, crossing the bridge over the tracks and heading up the sloping streets to the castle. He followed the cobbled road uphill, trying to ignore the fresh footprints in the snow all around him. The farther he traveled the more obvious it became that the things that had been hunting them the previous night must have numbered in their thousands. Every street was covered in their tracks.

"So where are they now?" Sam muttered to himself. It wasn't like the Voidborn to hide—they had no reason to, after all. So why did the city feel as if it had been abandoned?

Soon he arrived at the arched gate that was the main entrance to the castle. The imposing structure loomed over him, looking much larger than it had from the streets below. He passed under the arch and through the shattered remains of the heavy wooden gate that had presumably once sealed the entrance. He continued upward, heading through the second gatehouse and into the open courtyard beyond.

What he saw there was hard to believe.

Scattered around were the twisted shells of smashed Hunters and the gutted remains of several Grendels, all covered in a layer of snow. He had never seen anything like it. The Voidborn looked as if they'd been ripped to pieces. The burnt-out hulk of a drop-ship lay in what had once been a grand-looking building on the other side of the area. The broad trail of destruction leading to the impact point made it clear that something had brought down the alien vessel, but there was no obvious indication what.

Sam unclipped his holster and pulled out his gun. Something about the grisly scene made him extremely nervous. Judging by the layer of snow that covered the wreckage, it had been several days at least since whatever had taken place here, but he wasn't going to take any chances. He walked up to the nearest fallen Hunter and rolled it over with his foot. The silvery skin of the creature was slashed in several places and the thick green slime that was the nearest thing the Voidborn had to blood had congealed in a large puddle beneath it.

He knelt down beside the Hunter and examined the tears in the Drone's skin more carefully, realizing that the wounds looked exactly like claw marks. He realized that there was only one possible explanation. The creatures that had attacked them the previous night had done this. That made no sense. If the creatures were

Voidborn, why had they attacked their own? Sam shook his head; it was just one more unanswered question to add to the ever-growing pile. He began to stand up, but suddenly felt something cold and sharp press against the back of his neck.

"Drop it," a girl's voice said behind him.

Sam slowly placed his pistol on the ground.

"Stand," the voice said, and Sam slowly got to his feet. He turned around and let out an involuntary gasp. The girl standing opposite him, knife raised, looked about the same age as him, but that was where the similarities ended. Her skin was pale and covered in the same thick black veins as the creatures that had attacked them the previous night, and each of her fingers was tipped by a translucent claw. Her eyes were hidden behind a pair of dark sunglasses and she was wearing a black top with its hood pulled up over her head.

"Who are you?" the girl asked. "And what are you doing here?"

"My name's Sam," he replied, keeping his open palms out to his sides in what he hoped was a non-threatening gesture. "I'm sort of lost."

"You got that right," the girl replied. "You shouldn't be here."

"I know," Sam replied. "I'm trying to find a way home."

"And where's that exactly?" she asked, knife still raised.

"London," Sam replied, "I'm from London."

The girl didn't speak for a moment. She just stood there and studied him.

"Where are the others?" she eventually asked.

"What others?" Sam replied.

"Don't treat me like an idiot," the girl replied. "I've been following you since you reached the city. I saw them leave onboard one of those things." She gestured toward the downed drop-ship. "Only realized that you'd been left behind when you emerged from your hidey-hole this morning. You were lucky. Never seen anyone get away from the Vore before."

"The Vore?" Sam said. "Is that what you call those things?"

"Aye, it's short for carnivore," the girl replied, "and trust me when I say that's an appropriate name. Problem is that right now you're standing right on top of the biggest nest of them in the city. So I'm going to suggest we get out of here before they wake up. Stay in front of me and don't try anything." She gestured toward the gatehouse that led back outside. "Go on."

"I'm not going to hurt you, you know," Sam said as she picked his pistol up from the ground and tucked it into the back of her jeans.

"You're right," she replied, "you're not."

She followed him back to the street outside and together they began to walk down the hill, the girl staying several yards behind Sam at all times.

"Where are we going?" Sam asked after a couple of minutes of walking in silence.

"Anywhere but here," the girl replied. "It's only a few more hours till sunset, and when the Vore catch your scent—and they *will* catch your scent—they'll hunt you relentlessly until you're dead."

"How far away do we have to get?" Sam asked, glancing nervously up at the sky.

"About two miles out from the nest at least," the girl replied.

"They can't really track us from that far away, can they?" Sam asked.

"Oh, they can and they will," the girl replied. "How do you think I found you and your friends in the first place? One of the perks of my . . . condition."

"What happened to you?" Sam said. "If you don't mind me asking."

"I have no idea," the girl replied. "I woke up alone in an empty warehouse looking like this. That was a couple of months ago. Since then I've been concentrating on staying alive."

"I know the feeling," Sam said. "So what happened to the Voidborn?"

"The what?" the girl replied.

"The aliens, those things that were scattered all over the courtyard back there," Sam explained. "They're called the Voidborn. They've taken the entire planet and enslaved nearly everyone. There are just a few of us trying to fight back. That's why we were here in the first place, looking for any other people who might still have their free will."

"So why are you working with them?" the girl asked. "I saw the ship your friends left in."

"We're not working with the Voidborn," Sam said. "We managed to capture one of their Motherships and now it's under our control."

"How did you pull that off?"

"It's a long story."

"I'm not going anywhere," the girl replied.

Over the next half hour Sam recounted the story of his desperate fight to survive after the initial Voidborn invasion and his subsequent recruitment by the resistance and their victory in London. When he had finished, the girl said nothing for several minutes.

"So I was one of these Sleepers for nearly two years," the girl said, struggling to wrap her head around what he had just told her. Sam realized that when she had awoken there wouldn't have been anything to tell this girl how much time had passed while she'd been a Voidborn slave.

"I'm afraid so," Sam replied. "We've tried to wake the Sleepers in London, but it didn't work. As far as we know, you're the only person who's ever woken from the Voidborn sleep."

"Yeah, well you might have noticed I'm not quite the girl I used to be," she replied. "That could have something to do with it."

"We have people working on waking everyone back in London," Sam said. "If we could contact my friends, you could come back with us and maybe they can do something to help you."

"Not terribly keen on the idea of being a lab rat," the girl replied. "Let's just concentrate on getting you out of here in one piece for now."

Sam gave a quick nod. She was right—they had other priorities right now.

"Can I ask your name?" Sam asked after a couple more minutes of walking in silence.

"Maggie," the girl replied, "but you can call me Mag—everyone does, or should I say *did*."

"So you've not seen any sign of the Voidborn?" Sam asked.

"Other than those few you saw in the castle courtyard, no," Mag replied. "Oh, and that big ship floating above the castle on the day of the invasion."

Stirling had been right, Sam thought to himself. There had been a Mothership here. So where had it gone and, more to the point, when and why had it left?

"We need to move faster," Mag said, glancing up at the sky. "I want to be farther away from the main nest before it gets dark."

As the sun began to set, they found themselves walking through a quiet suburb of the city. Sam had gotten very used to the night's cloak of darkness being an ally over the past couple of years, but here it was something to fear. Mag had finally sheathed her knife just a few minutes earlier, having obviously decided that Sam did not pose much of a threat, though she had not returned his gun. Sam didn't ask for it back, not wanting to do anything to jeopardize what little trust she might have in him.

"We should shelter for the night in one of these houses," Mag said, looking at the comfortable detached homes that surrounded them, sniffing the air. "I don't think there are any Vore around here, but we'd still be better off staying out of the open."

"I could do with resting for a while anyway," Sam said. The wound in his side was throbbing. He needed to clean it and apply a fresh dressing if he wanted to reduce the chances of infection.

"That one looks good," he said, pointing at a slightly larger house that was set farther back from the road than the others. The wide expanse of lawn that surrounded the house would give anyone on watch good sight lines.

Mag gave a quick nod and the pair of them walked up the long driveway leading to the front door. The heavy wooden door was firmly locked.

"I'll try around the back," Sam said.

"No need," Mag said. She grabbed the door handle and

pushed, shattering the doorframe around the lock effort-lessly. "Not just a pretty face," she added, holding the door open for Sam. Clearly it was not just her appearance that she shared with the Vore, but at least some of their inhu-man strength too. Sam realized that if he had attacked her she would have been able to subdue him effortlessly.

As they entered the gloomy hallway of the house, Mag removed the sunglasses that she had been wearing all day and Sam finally saw her jet-black eyes. She caught him staring at her and gave him a slight smile.

"Not a fan of bright lights anymore, I'm afraid," Mag said, pulling back her hood to reveal her long, white hair. "At least it can't kill me like it can the Vore."

"So that's why they don't hunt during the day," Sam said. "They can't."

"Exactly," Mag replied. "Come on, let's see if we can find anything to eat."

They headed deeper into the house and Sam struggled to find his way through the darkened rooms, arms out-stretched to avoid walking into anything. Mag was clearly having no such problems, suited as she obviously was to a nocturnal life. She found the large open-plan kitchen at the back of the house and rooted through the drawers and cupboards. After a minute or two there was the sound of someone striking a match and Mag lit a large church candle on the countertop.

"Thanks," Sam said as he sat down on one of the high

stools at the breakfast bar. "Not as good in the dark as you are."

Mag placed a couple of cans of apricots on the counter and a tin of corned beef. They ate in silence for the next couple of minutes.

"I haven't thanked you," Sam said as he ate a spoonful of syrup-covered apricot.

"For what?" Mag asked.

"For getting me out of the city center," Sam replied. "If it hadn't been for you, I might have just holed up for the night somewhere near that nest. I'd have made pretty easy pickings if it hadn't been for you."

"Don't worry about it," Mag said. "I've seen what those things can do to people. It's not pretty."

"What people?" Sam asked with a frown. "I thought you said that you'd never found any sleepers in the city."

"The soldiers," Mag said. "They used to come into the city at night, but the Vore soon put a stop to that."

"What soldiers?" Sam asked urgently. "Where do they come from?"

"Dunno," Mag said with a shrug. "I stay clear of them now. I've seen them shoot other people like me and take them away in their helicopters. There used to be a few of us; now there's just me. They stuck together—it made them too easy to find. I've always preferred to go solo, seems safer that way. The soldiers are bad news—trust me."

"We have to try and find them," Sam said. He didn't

tell her how much she reminded him of himself when he had been alone in London after the invasion. He too had believed it was better to hide. It was only later that he had learned to fight.

"Did you not hear what I just said?" Mag asked, frowning.

"You don't understand," Sam said. "Those soldiers must be the ones who made the transmission that brought us up here in the first place. If I can get my hands on whatever radio equipment they're using, I can get in touch with my friends in London and they can come and collect us."

"I'm not going anywhere," Mag said, shaking her head. "The Vore are no threat to me. I leave them alone and they leave me alone."

"That's how I used to feel, but I learned that you can do more than just survive," Sam said. "You can join us and help take the fight to the Voidborn."

"No thanks," Mag said. "I'll take you to the western edge of the city, then you're on your own. That's the direction the soldiers usually come from. If you keep walking, I'm sure you'll bump into them eventually."

Mag put down her fork and quickly sniffed the air.

"You're bleeding again," she said. "You'd better go patch yourself up. If I can smell it, so can the Vore."

Sam finished the last of the apricots in the can, finally silencing his growling belly, and took the candle through to the dining room next door. By the candle's flickering light, he unclipped his combat harness before removing his jacket and T-shirt, one side of which was now wet with fresh blood. He walked over to the large wall-mounted mirror and gingerly pulled the field dressing off the gash in his side. Blood trickled from the deep cut and ran down his skin. The wound needed stitches, not a field dressing, but for the moment he would have to make do with what he had. He reached into his pack and removed one of the handful of dressings that remained in the first-aid kit. He carefully applied the self-adhesive pad as Mag walked into the room.

"Here," she said, placing a roll of bandage on the table and some painkillers. "Found these upstairs, thought you could use them."

"You couldn't give me a hand, could you?" Sam asked as he held the dressing in place beneath his left arm. He suddenly realized that she was staring at him with a puzzled expression. He looked down and saw what it was that had surprised her. He held his gleaming golden forearm and hand out in front of him, flexing the fingers. "Sorry, should have mentioned it earlier. Just a little souvenir of our last battle with the Voidborn."

"Can I?" She reached out to touch the metal.

"Be my guest," Sam said, holding his arm out to her.

Mag gently ran her clawed fingers over the golden surface. It was warm, and subtle sparkling trails were left in the surface where she had touched.

"It feels alive," Mag said.

"It is, in a way," Sam said. "I don't really understand how it works, to be honest, but it seems to behave itself most of the time."

"Doesn't it worry you?" Mag asked. "After everything you've told me about the Voidborn, do you really want their technology to be part of your body like this?"

"Hey, it's this or no arm at all," Sam said with a shrug. "I try not to think about it too much. I'm more worried about the Voidborn tech up here." He tapped the side of his head.

"And that's what kept you awake when the Voidborn came," Mag said.

"Yeah, lucky old me," Sam replied with a crooked smile. There had been moments over the last two years when he had wondered if the Sleepers weren't the lucky ones in a way. At least they didn't have to face the nightmare of living in a world overrun by the Voidborn.

Mag helped Sam wrap the bandage tightly around his chest, pressing the dressing firmly against his injured side. He winced slightly at the pressure on the wound, but he knew it would help staunch any further bleeding. If the Vore were still on their trail, that might turn out to be the difference between life and death.

"I'll go and see if I can find a clean top," Mag said. "You should burn that." She gestured to the blood-soaked T-shirt on the table.

A few minutes later Sam pulled his jacket back on over

the clean, if much too large, T-shirt that Mag had found upstairs. He tossed the bloody shirt into the kitchen sink and Mag passed him a small tin of lighter fluid. He squirted the clear liquid over the shirt and tossed a lit match onto the sodden cloth. It went up with a flash, the flickering flames lighting up the room for a couple of minutes before fading away to nothing.

"That's better," Mag said, sniffing the air. All that Sam could smell was the smoke from the burning cloth, so he decided to take her word for it that he was no longer a walking dinner invitation for the Vore.

"You should get some sleep," Mag said. "You have a long walk ahead of you tomorrow."

# 4

"You okay?" Jay asked Rachel. He had found her sitting on the trunk of a car near the ruins of Big Ben, staring into the distance.

"Not really," she replied with a sigh.

"Me neither," Jay said, sitting down beside her. "I can't help wondering if I'd just held on to Sam a bit better he might not have fallen. I can't get the look on his face out of my head."

"It's not your fault, Jay," Rachel said, putting her hand on his knee. "It's no one's fault but theirs." She pointed up at the colossal Mothership hovering above them.

"I know." Jay stared at the ground. "Doesn't stop me wondering *what if*, though."

"We didn't . . . we couldn't have known what we were walking into," Rachel said, shaking her head. "Who knows what other new horrors the Voidborn are cooking up for us?"

"I don't want to think about that at the moment," Jay replied, "but I tell you this—I'd rather take on a Grendel solo than face another swarm of those things."

"I suppose you've had Stirling grilling you too," Rachel said.

"Yeah, I think he'd quite like us to go back and get him a live sample."

"Don't think he'll get many volunteers for that mission," Rachel replied. Sam's death had knocked everyone in the group's morale. It had never been formally decided, but they had regarded Sam as the leader of the group. After all, without him they would now either be dead or still hiding in a hole in the ground. His sudden loss had come as a devastating blow to everyone.

"Hell, it's just another bug-eyed Voidborn freak," Jay said. "What more does he need to know?"

"He's just worried," Rachel said. "To be honest, I am too. You saw how many of those things there were—what happens if the Voidborn release more of them here?"

"Then we'll beat them back," Jay said. "As long as we've got our own pet Voidborn, we've got an advantage that no amount of those freaks can offset."

"I hope you're right," Rachel replied, "because I don't want to know what would happen if a swarm of those things found a building full of Sleepers."

"I know what you mean," Jay said, flashing back in his head to the horrifying sight of the thousands of creatures swarming up the sides of the department store in Edinburgh. "It's weird. The Hunters and the Grendels are bad enough, but at least they always felt like they were under some sort of control. Those things up in Edinburgh, man . . . that was just bloodthirsty chaos. It's as if the Voidborn don't care about whether or not they could control those things. They're like a force of nature."

"Scorched earth," Rachel said quietly.

"What?"

"It's something that Jackson once taught me," Rachel said, remembering the words of the ex-marine who had trained them all to fight before heroically giving his own life to save theirs. "An army in retreat will destroy everything as they fall back to make sure that there's nothing left for the enemy to use. Humans used to be really good at it—maybe the Voidborn are the same."

"You think they're just going to wipe us out?" Jay asked with a frown. "If that's true, why didn't they do it when they arrived? There's nothing anyone could have done to stop them."

"Perhaps," Rachel said, "but maybe that's the point. There was no need to wipe us out when we're no threat to them, but if we become a threat by, say, capturing one of their Motherships, maybe we've gone too far and they'll just wipe out everyone in the country. Let's face it, what's one little island worth when you have the whole of the rest of the world in the palm of your hand?"

"There are easier ways to destroy us, surely," Jay said, shaking his head. "You can't tell me that machines with the intelligence and power of the Voidborn don't have nukes or something like that."

"I suppose," Rachel said, staring at the shattered remains of the massive clock tower on the other side of the square, "but if that's true, why haven't they used them?"

"No idea," Jay said with a shrug. "Who knows how they think? Come on back to the compound—it's freezing out here."

"Give me a minute," Rachel said. "I won't be long."

Jay looked at her for a moment, studying her face. "Okay," he said, "don't make me send a Grendel out here after you."

She gave him a weak smile and watched him walk up the road toward St. James's Park. She turned back to the ruined Houses of Parliament and recalled the time they had finally confronted the Voidborn in the skies above London. If it hadn't been for Sam, they would all have died that day. Now he and his unique connection to the Voidborn were gone, along with perhaps their only hope of ever achieving such a spectacular victory again.

Sam woke with a start, feeling a hand press down on his mouth. His eyes shot open and he looked up at the shadowy figure of Mag, a single finger pressed to her lips. She pointed down at the bedroom floor and a moment later

Sam heard a crash from somewhere beneath them.

"Vore, two or three of them," she whispered. "We have to go, quick and quiet." She reached around to the small of her back and pulled out Sam's pistol, passing it to him. "Don't use it unless you absolutely have to."

Sam gave a nod and climbed off the bed as Mag moved over to the bedroom window. She lifted the catch and swung the window open slowly. Sam looked down at the shrubs below.

"When you hit the ground, run," Mag whispered. "Don't look back."

Sam nodded and climbed carefully up onto the window sill before turning and lowering himself backward out of the window, dropping the last few feet to the ground. He raised his pistol, straining to spot any sign of movement in the dark shadows of the surrounding garden before setting off across the snowy lawn at a sprint. Mag dropped down behind him and hit the ground running, catching up with him effortlessly.

"Faster," she whispered. She was picking up the scent of more Vore nearby, lots of them.

Sam tried to increase his pace, but his battered, exhausted body had nearly reached its limits, even with the adrenaline pumping through his veins. They reached the road a few seconds later, pounding through the snow as a series of blood-curdling screeching howls filled the night air.

Suddenly, a bush to Sam's right seemed to explode as a Vore burst from it, claws outstretched. The monstrous creature hit him hard, slamming him to the ground and knocking the wind out of him. Sam struggled desperately, trying to push the creature off him, gasping in pain as he felt its razor-sharp claws stabbing into his shoulder. The Vore's mouth opened wide. It was too strong and Sam felt a moment of pure mortal terror as its fetid breath washed over his face.

Mag fell on the Vore like an animal, her own claws raking across the charcoal-colored skin of the creature's back, leaving long, gaping wounds. The wounded Vore turned on her with a pained howl, releasing Sam and staggering to its feet as Mag sprang toward it again. She knocked the creature to the ground, flat on its back, her razor-sharp teeth snapping closed on its exposed throat with a grisly crunch. The creature thrashed helplessly for a moment and then lay still. Sam backed away from Mag as she turned toward him with a feral hiss, the creature's black blood covering her face. He heard another roar from behind him and turned to see at least a dozen Vore galloping on all fours down the moonlit street toward him.

"Run!" Mag growled. Sam did not need to be told twice. He turned and sprinted down the road, nothing in his head now other than the animal instinct to survive. He felt a moment of pure dread as the road fifty yards ahead of them was suddenly filled with more charging Vore. There was nowhere left to go. Sam raised his pistol and fired at the nearest creature, the impact of the bullets barely seeming to slow it. He kept firing and eventually the creature staggered and fell as the hammer of his pistol hit an empty chamber with a final click. Mag rounded on the advancing creatures, a low guttural growl coming from her throat. Strong as she was, Sam knew there was no way she could ever hope to keep them all at bay.

Suddenly, the advancing Vore at one end of the street were simply gone, swallowed in an enormous ball of fire. The light of the explosion was impossibly bright, the concussion wave that accompanied the thunderous noise knocking both Sam and Mag clean off their feet. A few seconds later all that was left was a smoldering crater and the twisted burning wreckage of long-abandoned cars.

Sam's head spun, his ears ringing as he vainly tried to force himself back to his feet. The Vore at the other end of the street had stopped, momentarily stunned by the brightness. They began to advance more cautiously, hissing and growling as they closed the distance to Sam and Mag. A sudden thunder of heavy gunfire shredded the front rank of advancing creatures in a hail of bullets. Sam flattened himself to the ground as the air filled with the angry buzz of bullets flying just above his head. He tried to look back over his shoulder and saw the silhouettes of a dozen heavily armed men, picking their way through the burning debris of the explosion, weapons firing constantly. The Vore tried, at first, to continue their advance under the withering barrage of fire, but it was futile. Only a few seconds later the handful of surviving creatures scattered and ran in all directions as their own animal survival instincts kicked in.

Sam remained on the ground as the soldiers moved toward him and Mag, weapons still raised. Mag sprang to her feet and sprinted in the opposite direction, and Sam watched in horror as one of the soldiers pulled a handgun from the holster on his waist and fired. The round hit Mag squarely between the shoulder blades, and she slammed hard into the ground as her legs gave way beneath her.

"No," Sam said, watching her lifeless body fall, his voice little more than a hoarse croak. He staggered to his feet.

"This is Recon Echo," the nearest soldier spoke into his mic. "Predator strike on target. We've found the boy and taken down the hybrid. We're clear for extraction."

"Roger that, Echo," his radio crackled in response. "Helo inbound."

A few seconds later Sam could hear the distant thumping drone of helicopter rotors.

"You didn't have to kill her," Sam yelled angrily as the lead soldier advanced toward him.

"I know," the soldier replied, before raising the pistol again, leveling it at Sam's chest and pulling the trigger.

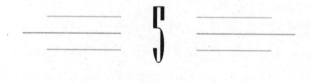

**5**

Sam's eyes flickered open, but the bright overhead light forced him to close them with a wince. He took a deep breath and slowly opened his eyes again, giving them time to adjust to the light. He was lying handcuffed to the steel frame of a bed in a bare concrete cell. He pulled fruitlessly at the shackle attached to his still human wrist. It was no good—he wasn't going anywhere.

He forced himself up into a sitting position. Now that the adrenaline had worn off he could feel every cut, bruise, and scrape that covered his body, but the truth was that he was relieved he could still feel anything at all. His last memory was of the soldier raising his weapon and pulling the trigger. He carefully lifted his T-shirt and looked down at his chest. There, just above his breastbone, was a circular burn, two inches across with a tiny puncture wound in the center. The pistol the soldier had shot him with must have fired some sort of non-lethal round. He realized with a sudden rush of relief that the soldier had used the same weapon on Mag, which meant that there was a chance at least that she was still alive. He lifted the dressing on the wound in his side and saw that it had been cleaned and then closed with a neat row of stitches.

"Hello!" Sam shouted. "Is anyone out there?" There was no response. He had no idea who had saved and then captured him, but at that point he had a thousand questions that needed answers. If they'd wanted him dead, they could have finished him earlier. The fact that he was still breathing meant they must value their captives a little at least.

A few minutes later there was the sound of a key turning in the door. A tall, athletic man with short gray hair, wearing urban camouflage fatigues, walked into the room carrying a metal folding chair. Attached to the side of the man's skull was a small black disc, which flickered with a sickly green light, clearly some form of Voidborn technology. He unfolded the chair and sat down on the opposite side of the room from Sam, studying his face for a moment before speaking.

"My name is Mason," the man said, "and I have a few questions for you."

"Where's Mag?" Sam demanded.

"Mag? Oh, you mean the hybrid we captured with you.

Don't worry, she's . . . secure," Mason replied.

"What do you mean?" Sam asked. "Where is she?"

"Traditionally the person handcuffed to the bed isn't the one who asks the questions," Mason replied. "My turn. Who are you?"

"My name's Sam," he replied after a moment or two. "Sam Riley."

"Well, Sam, there are a couple of things that I really need you to explain to me," Mason said, leaning forward in his chair. "For a start I'd like you to tell me why you have Voidborn technology replacing a large part of your right arm, and secondly I want to know what you have to do with the Voidborn drop-ship that our surveillance drones spotted over Edinburgh the night before last."

Voidborn . . . Mason had called them that without Sam telling him anything. Whoever this man was, he knew a certain amount about the invaders, but how?

"What if I don't feel like telling you anything," Sam said defiantly. "What then?"

"Then our conversation becomes more . . . impolite," Mason replied. "Do you know what the penalty is for collaboration during a time of war?"

"I'm not a collaborator," Sam snapped angrily.

"Really?" Mason replied. "Well, perhaps you'd like to explain how you got that, then." He gestured toward Sam's arm. "The Voidborn are not known for their generosity."

"You wouldn't believe me if I told you," Sam said, shaking his head.

"I think you'd be surprised what I'd believe," Mason replied. "So are you going to tell me or do I have to go and ask your hybrid friend much less politely?"

"You keep calling her that," Sam said. "What does it mean?"

"More questions," Mason said. "Still no answers, though. Oh well, plan B." He stood up and walked toward the door.

"Wait," Sam said with a sigh. "It's not exactly Voidborn technology. I lost my arm to a Voidborn nanite swarm during the battle to capture the Mothership over London."

"What?" Mason demanded, his face a sudden combination of surprise and disbelief.

"We captured the Mothership over London and during the fight I lost my arm," Sam said. "This just grew back to replace it. I have no idea why."

"You're seriously trying to tell me that you captured a Voidborn Mothership," Mason said, shaking his head. "That's impossible. You'd need an army."

"We had one," Sam replied. Something told him that it was not a good idea to tell Mason that the army in question had consisted of four kids and an old man.

"When was this supposed to have happened?" Mason asked with a frown.

"Three months ago," Sam replied. "London is ours."

"Until the Voidborn want it back," Mason said with a dismissive wave. "Do you have any idea how many Mother-ships there are? More than enough to wipe you from the face of the planet if they wanted to, Mothership or not."

"How come you know so much about them," Sam replied, "and why aren't you under their control? Or are you?"

"These things keep me and my men safe from the con-trol signal," Mason said, tapping the implant attached to the side of his head, "and the reason I know so much about them is that I used to work for them."

"You did *what?*"

"I used to work for them," Mason replied, sitting back down in the chair opposite Sam. "Not that I knew that at the time. I was, shall we say, an independent contractor. I had no idea who was really pulling all the strings behind the scenes. To be honest, I didn't really care."

"You were part of the Foundation," Sam said, "and you have the nerve to call *me* a collaborator."

The Foundation was a secretive organization that had been furthering the Voidborn's plans for thousands of years, steering human history and evolution to suit their masters' twisted ends. Sam had only learned of its exist-ence when Dr. Stirling had confessed to Sam that both he and Sam's father had worked as researchers for the organ-ization until they had learned the true horrors of what the alien machines were actually planning, and had decided to fight against them instead.

"How the hell do you know about the Foundation?" Mason demanded, his frown deepening.

"Because one of the people who used to work for the Foundation helped us take down the Mothership," Sam replied. "He told me all about it."

"Who was this man who helped you?" Mason demanded. "What was his name?"

"I don't think I can remember," Sam said with a smile. "Must be all the blows to the head over the past few days."

"This isn't a game, Sam," Mason said, shaking his head slightly. "You saw what the Voidborn have done to Edinburgh. What's to stop them doing that to London? Or the entire planet? If everything you've told me is true, then we're all on the same side. It's us versus them— there's not going to be any runner-up prizes."

"I know that," Sam replied, "I'm not stupid, but why should I trust you?"

"Because I saved your life," Mason replied. "I'm sure I don't need to remind you of the situation you were in when my men found you."

"Yeah, and then you brought me here and subtly suggested that you might torture me and my friend if I didn't tell you everything you want to know. So, really, you could look at this two different ways, couldn't you?"

"I thought you were working with the Voidborn," Mason said. "For all I know, you are and everything you've just told me is a lie. Trust works both ways."

"So if I give you the name of the man who helped us retake London, you'll let me go?" Sam asked.

"If you give me the right name," Mason replied.

"And if I give you the wrong name?"

"Then I drop you in the center of Edinburgh in the middle of the night and let nature take its course," Mason replied. The look on his face made it clear that he was not making idle threats.

"Stirling," Sam said after a moment, "his name is Stirling."

"Iain Stirling?" Mason said, a smile quickly replacing the frown. "Iain Stirling is the man working with you? I don't believe it. I assumed he'd been lost to the Voidborn."

"You two know each other, I take it."

"No, not really," Mason replied, "but the last mission I was given by the Foundation was to find him and kill him."

"*What?*" Sam said with a sudden look of shock on his face.

"I was one of the Foundation's most trusted security operatives," Mason said. "I had . . . certain skills that were useful to them. I had a talent for removing *problems.*"

"You mean you were an assassin," Sam said, staring back at him.

"If that's what you want to call it," Mason replied. "I never knew why the Foundation wanted people eliminated—I was not in the habit of questioning my orders. They were simply targets to me, nothing more. When Stirling betrayed the Foundation, I was given the task of hunting down him and another man called Daniel Shaw."

Mason saw the fleeting look of surprise on Sam's face.

"How do you know that name?" Mason asked.

"Stirling must have mentioned it," Sam lied.

"And you're not as good a liar as you think you are," Mason replied with a frown.

"I didn't know him as Daniel Shaw," Sam replied with a sigh. "I knew him as Andrew Riley. He was my dad."

"I'll be damned," Mason said, studying Sam's face carefully. "I don't see much of a resemblance."

"I was adopted," Sam said. A fact that he himself had only learned from Dr. Stirling recently.

"I see," Mason replied. "Well, it's a small world."

"What do you mean?" Sam asked.

"Until recently your father was here, working with us," Mason said.

"He's alive!" Sam said, feeling a sudden rush of excitement in his chest. "Where is he?"

"I have no idea, I'm afraid," Mason said with a slight frown. "We had a . . . disagreement. He left the base a couple of months ago."

"What was he doing here? Why were you working together?"

"As I mentioned before," Mason said, "years ago I was given the task of eliminating your father by the Foundation.

When I finally tracked him down, he was the one who first showed me incontrovertible evidence of what the Foundation really was and how it was furthering the Voidborn agenda on Earth prior to an invasion. Needless to say, that rather changed my opinion of my employers and I quickly realized I could never be a part of what they were planning. That was when I began to work secretly against the Foundation from within, smuggling out what Voidborn technology I could and delivering it into the hands of your father. He was working as part of a government initiative with Iain Stirling that was designed to prepare some sort of meaningful resistance when the Voidborn finally, inevitably, arrived."

"And you have no idea where he is now?" Sam said.

"No, I'm sorry," Mason replied, shaking his head. "After the Voidborn released the creatures in Edinburgh I was determined that we should do something to help them, but your father disagreed. He thought it was a waste of our resources."

"Help them?" Sam said, looking confused. "What do you mean?"

"The creatures that infest the city," Mason said, "they're not Voidborn constructs. They're human, or at least they once were."

"Oh my God," Sam said, feeling suddenly sick to his stomach. "You mean, those things were . . ."

"The former inhabitants of the city, yes," Mason replied.

"When the Voidborn Mothership left, those things began to appear all over the center of the city at night. At first we thought they were just some new form of Voidborn weapon, but when we eventually captured specimens your father quickly realized that they were mutated humans. We still don't know what the Voidborn did to them, but we did know that their numbers were increasing all the time as more and more of the Voidborn-controlled humans that were left behind were transformed into those things. The creatures can spread the infection that causes their mutation through their bite; just one of them could turn an entire group of Voidborn-controlled humans in just a matter of hours."

"So the Sleepers became the Vore," Sam said quietly, still struggling to get his head around the true horrifying scale of what Mason was describing.

"The Vore?"

"That's what Mag called them," Sam said, shaking his head. "She was a Sleeper too, but then she woke up looking the way she does now, with no memory of what had happened."

"She was lucky," Mason said, "though it may not seem like it. For the vast majority of the humans the Voidborn left behind, the transformation was total, but a handful of the survivors were only partially altered. The degree of transformation varies. Some of the hybrids are more human than others. The girl you were brought in with is one of the very few who retained some semblance of their former humanity."

"And my dad didn't think it was worth trying to help them," Sam said with a frown. "That doesn't sound like him."

"Your father thought the priority was defeating the Voidborn," Mason said. "The way he saw it, it was point-less to try and treat the symptoms of the disease: you have to cure the disease itself. I suppose it was a more scientific way of looking at things. Who knows, maybe he was right. We've had no success with trying to treat the converted humans . . . the Vore as you call them."

Sam sat in silence for a minute, trying to absorb the enormity of what Mason had told him. The Voidborn had always seemed to want to preserve the enslaved masses of humanity, for whatever reason, but this was something altogether different and more horrible. He had a sudden horrific vision of London overrun by the Vore, his friends being swallowed up by a ravenous tide of glistening teeth and claws.

"Are they spreading?" Sam asked.

"Yes," Mason said with a nod, "but slowly, and we're doing our best to find a way to stop them from leaving the city."

"So, where are we now?" Sam asked, looking at the bare concrete walls that surrounded him.

"Two hundred yards below Faslane naval base," Mason

replied, "about twenty-five miles west of Glasgow."

"I need to contact my people in London," Sam said. "I have to let them know I'm still alive."

"I think the best thing would be if we were to take you back ourselves," Mason replied after a moment's thought. "If everything you've told me is true, then I need to see it for myself."

"Fair enough," Sam replied. The addition of Mason's men and resources to their own could be a great help. A nagging voice at the back of his head told him there was more that Mason wasn't telling him, but he supposed that it would take time for proper trust to develop between them. Besides which he didn't have much choice. He was, after all, the one handcuffed to the bed. "I just have one condition: I want to see Mag first."

The cell door swung open and Mag hissed in discomfort as the overhead light flickered on, retreating into the farthest corner from the door.

"It's okay, it's me," Sam said as he stepped into the room. He turned back toward the soldier beside the door. "Turn the lights off."

The soldier beside the door glanced over at Mason, who gave a quick nod, and he flicked the switch next to the door. Mag was still visible in the dim light that shone through the doorway from the corridor beyond, huddled in the corner.

"Are you okay?" Sam asked quietly, walking into the

cell and squatting down in front of her. She slowly lifted her head and looked up at him.

"Aye, I'm okay," she replied with a nod. "No thanks to those morons." She gestured at Mason and the two soldiers standing in the corridor.

"You're going to have to take my word for this," Sam said, "but I think they may actually be on our side."

"They've got a funny way of showing it," Mag replied, scowling at the men outside.

"I've persuaded them to let you go," Sam said. "Think you'll be able to behave yourself?"

"You mean am I going to rip anyone's throat out?" Mag asked, looking Sam straight in the eye.

Sam tried to ignore the memory of her blood-soaked face from the previous night.

"You saved my life," Sam replied. "You did what you had to."

"Perhaps," Mag said, looking down at the floor. "I hate it when I lose control like that. Reminds me of who I really am now."

"That's not you," Sam said. "The Vore might be a part of you, but the human part is still in control."

"For now," Mag said with a sigh.

"Come on," Sam said, "Mason and his men are going to take me back to London and I wondered if you'd like to come with us?"

"I'd just like to be released," Mag said. "I told you before I don't want to be part of your war."

"You don't have to be," Sam said, "but London is safe, for the moment at least. A lot safer than staying around here, trust me."

She shook her head. "I'm sorry, Sam," she said. "I don't think I'm ever really going to fit in anywhere again. Thanks for the offer, but I'll make my own way."

"It's your call," Sam said. "I'll talk to Mason."

"Thanks," Mag replied.

Sam walked back over to where Mason stood, flanked by the two soldiers.

"She wants to be released," Sam said to Mason, glancing back into the cell where Mag was standing in the shadows, eyes fixed on them.

"I'm not sure that's a good idea," Mason replied. "It's not going to get any safer out there, you know."

"I think she can look after herself," Sam said with a crooked smile.

"Yes, I suppose she can," Mason replied. "Very well, I'll have her escorted to the base perimeter."

"I'd like to see her off," Sam said. "I owe her a proper good-bye."

"I understand." Mason turned to the soldier beside him. "Escort them both to gate three and return the girl's belongings."

The soldier gave a quick nod.

"Come on," Sam said, stepping inside the cell, "they're letting you go."

Mag walked out of the cell, her hand shielding her eyes from the overhead lights in the corridor. She looked at Mason for a moment, a slight frown on her face, before the soldier gestured for her and Sam to follow him down the corridor. They entered a wire cage elevator at the end and stood in silence as it trundled upward for what seemed like ages. Eventually the heavy steel doors rumbled apart and they found themselves in a huge parking garage lined with trucks painted in a drab military green. Another soldier approached carrying Mag's hooded top and backpack.

A few minutes later they were walking across the large open area outside the garage toward a gate guarded by a pair of armed guards in a watchtower.

"Be careful with that man," Mag said quietly as they approached, "the tall one."

"You mean Mason?" Sam asked.

"Yes, the one in charge," Mag said. "There's something off about him."

"What do you mean?" Sam asked.

"I don't know," Mag said with a shake of the head. "Just something not quite right."

"Don't worry," Sam said. "Once we get to London we'll be fine. I don't think he really believes what I'm telling him. When he see the Mothership and that it is actually under our control, I think he'll relax a little."

"Maybe," Mag replied, "just keep an eye on him."

"I will," Sam said. "I'll be careful."

The soldier who had been leading them waved to the guards in the tower and a couple of seconds later the heavy gates began to roll apart. Mag turned toward Sam and surprised him by giving him a quick hug.

"Thanks," she said as she pulled away.

"For what?" Sam asked with a smile.

"For not treating me like a monster."

"You're not a monster, Mag," Sam said, shaking his head.

"I'm not sure everyone would agree with you," she replied with a sad smile. "Good-bye, Sam."

Sam watched as Mag walked away down the road, the gates rumbling closed again as she vanished from view.

"How many men have you got?" Sam asked as he looked down into the submarine pen.

"Nearly forty combat troops and a handful of scientific staff," Mason replied. "They're still working on a way to reverse the effects of whatever it is that the Voidborn have done in Edinburgh. They're doing the best they can, but without your father's help progress has been slow. He may have been difficult to work with at times, but he was a brilliant man."

Sam had always known that his father had been engaged in some kind of secretive work for the government, but it was only recently that he had discovered how closely he had been involved with the ongoing fight against the Voidborn and their human representatives on Earth, the Foundation.

"Do you really have absolutely no idea where he went?" Sam asked. It was unbelievably frustrating to have missed him by a matter of weeks. At the very least he had the consolation of knowing that he was still alive. That was more than could be said for his mother and sister, who he had not seen since the day of the Voidborn invasion. He told himself that they were safe somewhere in London under the care of the Voidborn that were now under Sam's control, but he had no real proof. For a long time he'd tried hard not to think about his family, instead focusing on the fight against the Voidborn, but suddenly learning that his father was alive and awake brought a lot of those suppressed emotions bubbling up to the surface.

The truth of it was that he wasn't sure what he would say to his father, a man who, after all, had lied to him for as long as he could remember. A man who had implanted Sam and numerous other children with unproven alien technology. For Sam, though, the hardest lie to accept was the fact that his mother and father were not his biological parents and that he'd had to learn that from someone else. He still thought of Andrew Riley as his father, not Daniel Shaw, even though they were, of course, one and the same person.

"No, I'm afraid not, Sam," Mason replied with a sad expression on his face. "He walked out of the main gate with a rifle and a month's supplies. I wish he could have stayed, but our differences became irreconcilable."

"So was it him that designed those things?" Sam asked, pointing at the glowing green implant on the side of Mason's head.

"Yes," Mason replied, touching the device, "it took him months working with the tiny amount of Voidborn tech that we had managed to smuggle out of the Foundation before the invasion. This facility was con-structed under Faslane by the government and was one of only two in the country. The other, as you're no doubt aware, was in London and had served as the research hub where Shaw and Stirling carried out their work to protect us against the Voidborn. This facility was designed to serve as a permanent garrison that would be immune to Voidborn control in the event of a Voidborn invasion and from which we might be able to mount some form of concerted resistance.

"Unfortunately, as you probably already know, the Voidborn caught us off-guard. They arrived far earlier than even our most pessimistic projections had sug-gested. This place was supposed to have at least one fully trained submarine crew and a nuclear submarine with a full complement of Trident missiles. As it was, we had a pair of pilots, two squads of marines, and a handful of scientists when the Voidborn arrived. We were hopelessly unprepared, trapped in the shielded bunker below us with no way of leaving without falling victim to the enemy's control signal.

"That was when your father arrived. He had been unable to reach the London facility on the day of the invasion due to the sheer number of Voidborn units there and so he headed for the only other place he knew where there might be humans who had not been enslaved. Here."

"That's a hell of a walk," Sam said with a frown.

"It was," Mason replied, "but your father is a remarkable man, Sam. There aren't many people who could have made a journey like that, especially through occupied territory. Nevertheless, it took him weeks. I have to confess that by the time he arrived I had almost given up hope. As soon as he got here, he took control of the scientific team and, after a year of painful trial and error, he had developed these." Mason tapped the device attached to his skull. "For the first time, we could leave the facility to assess exactly how dire the situation was. We don't need the devices while we're inside the bunker, but if we want to go topside we have to use them or we'd be just as vulnerable to the control signal as anyone else. Until you arrived we had no idea that anyone had escaped the Voidborn in London. It was assumed to be a total loss. We didn't know there was anyone there mounting a concerted resistance, much less that they would be able to take control of a Voidborn Mothership—something which, frankly, I still find hard to believe."

"Yeah, well, you'll get to see it for yourself soon enough," Sam replied, looking down at the soldiers who were busily packing their gear into backpacks and checking their weapons.

"I hope so," Mason said, his expression suddenly turning cold, "because if you're lying to me and I find out that you're leading us into a Voidborn trap I'll kill you myself. Understood?"

"Understood," Sam said, swallowing nervously. He tried very hard not to think about the number of bodies that undoubtedly littered Mason's past.

"We leave as soon as it gets dark," Mason said. "We're reasonably certain that the Motherships over Edinburgh and London were the only ones stationed over the UK mainland, but I'd rather not bump into any unexpected visitors in daylight." Mason turned and looked down at the men preparing their equipment below. "I need to brief my men. If I were you, I'd take the opportunity to clean yourself up and grab something to eat."

Sam watched as Mason walked away. He knew it was a risk taking Mason and his men into London, given how little he actually knew about him, but, at some point at least, his father had trusted him and that counted for something. They may have fallen out over what to do about the Vore, but they were all on the same side in this. They had to be. Despite all that, as he turned back to look at the men in the room below, Mag's parting words still nagged at him.

*Keep an eye on him.*

Sam intended to do exactly that.

# 6

Sam walked toward the Chinook helicopter, its huge double rotors already slicing through the air. Mason strode up the ramp to the interior, which was lit with blood-red light, swiftly followed by a dozen of his men who quickly stowed their gear and took their seats along the bulkheads. Sam followed, past the soldier manning the mounted heavy machine gun, and found himself a spare seat. The men moved with the practiced efficiency of professional soldiers, barely glancing at Sam as he watched them finish their final preparations for take-off. A minute or so later, Mason finished talking to the pilots and turned to address his men.

"Gentlemen, you should consider this a combat drop," Mason said. "Until we have firm evidence to the contrary we are going to work on the assumption that London is still in the hands of the enemy. You all conducted scouting missions into Edinburgh while the enemy Mothership was stationed there so I'm sure I don't need to remind you of the dangers we may face. We have plotted a course to avoid the Voidborn control nodes that may still be active en route, which should mean we don't run into any of their airborne units, but you should still be ready for an emergency landing at any time."

Sam and the others had done exactly the same thing on their way north. The Voidborn Motherships may have gone, but the automated control nodes that allowed the Hunter Drones to operate semi-autonomously and continue to care for the millions of Sleepers up and down the country were still active. Sam thought back to the first time he had seen one of the nodes in the middle of the field in Wembley Stadium surrounded by thousands of dormant Sleepers. They had learned the hard way that the Hunters would aggressively defend a node if it were attacked, turning from nursemaids to savage killers in the blink of an eye.

"Any questions?" Mason asked. "No? Good. Flight time should be just over two hours."

Mason walked through the cabin to where Sam was sitting and looked down at him.

"Once we arrive these two gentlemen will be taking care of you." Mason gestured to the two grim-faced soldiers that sat on either side of him. "You are not to leave their sight. Understood?"

For a fleeting second Sam wanted to tell Mason that he was more than capable of looking after himself, given everything he'd been through since the invasion, but he decided that it probably wasn't worth it at that precise moment. From Mason's perspective he was just a kid after all, and Sam tried very hard not to smile at the thought of his face when he realized that "kid" had command of an army of tame Voidborn.

"Don't worry," Sam replied, "I won't go wandering off."

Mason walked back to the front of the compartment and took a seat next to the bulkhead that separated the cockpit from the passenger compartment. A few seconds later the thumping rumble of the rotors increased in intensity and the massive machine slowly lifted into the air. Sam watched as the lights of the base disappeared from view to be replaced by the pitch blackness of the post-invasion night. The next time his feet touched the ground he would be home.

Mag squatted on the corner of the roof of one of the darkened buildings that surrounded the landing pad. It had not been difficult to evade the guards patroling the perimeter. Over the last couple of months she had become extremely adept at avoiding detection by anyone or anything. She watched as the helicopter with Sam on board lifted into the air and disappeared over the horizon. She had wanted to make sure that he had departed safely. He had been the only person that she had spent any time with since she had awoken to find herself transformed. The fact was he had made her feel human again and she realized now that she had almost forgotten how that felt.

She'd been more than a half mile away from the base before she'd turned back. The nagging memory of Mason's scent had made her return. He didn't smell right; she couldn't put her finger on exactly what was wrong about him, but she had learned to trust her heightened senses. They had saved her life on more than one occasion.

She was just about to head back off the base when the hangar doors on the opposite side of the landing pad began to rumble slowly open. She watched as a second helicopter, identical to the one in which Sam had just left, was towed out onto the pad by a small tractor-like vehicle. Mag frowned slightly as two soldiers walked out of the hangar, flanking a figure wearing wrist and leg shackles, with a black bag over their head. The soldiers pushed the prisoner up the loading ramp and a few seconds later the helicopter started to lift off. However, instead of pulling away it hovered in place above the pad. Then Mag noticed the cables dangling from the cargo hook on the machine's belly.

A moment later the tractor reappeared towing a trailer with a large steel crate on the back of it. As the trailer drew to a halt beneath the helicopter, more soldiers ran out from the hangar and attached the cables to mounts on top of the crate. Suddenly there was a loud metallic clang from the crate as something slammed against the walls inside.

Mag felt a cold sensation in the pit of her stomach as the scent hit her nostrils.

The unmistakeable animal stench of the Vore.

The soldiers quickly finished attaching the cables and one of them gave a thumbs-up to the pilot, whose head was just visible, poking out of the cockpit window above them. A moment later the crate lifted up off the trailer, swinging beneath the massive helicopter like a pendulum as it began to climb into the air. Mag made a split-second decision as the helicopter began to turn toward her, heading for the perimeter fence. She leaped to her feet, sprinting across the gravel roof of the building, picking up speed. The crate passed by ten feet above her and she leaped with all her newfound animal strength, slamming into the side with a bang, her claws fighting for purchase on the hard surface. She grabbed desperately for the top edge of the crate as the helicopter cleared the perimeter fence and began to pick up speed. There was a moment of panic as Mag felt herself starting to lose her grip, and she gave a low bestial growl, using every ounce of her strength to pull herself up. She flattened herself to the top of the steel box, holding tight to the cable mounts as the wind speed increased. She realized she had no idea where the helicopter was headed or why they were transporting live Vore, but her gut told her that it was no coincidence that they had taken off straight after the helicopter carrying Sam. She closed her eyes against the stinging high-speed winds, praying that she would have the strength to hang on long enough for them to reach their destination, wherever that may be.

Rachel squeezed the trigger, the butt of her rifle kicking hard against her shoulder. The short burst tore a neat hole in the center of the paper target at the other end of the firing range. In her mind's eye the target was one of the nightmarish creatures they'd discovered in Edinburgh, charging toward her and then cut down in the hail of her bullets. She had finally given in to Dr. Stirling's repeated requests for more information about the things, but reliving the memories of that night had left her feeling angry and frustrated. She had always found the firing range an excellent means of stress relief, but even that wasn't really working today. Nat approached as Rachel emptied her clip and placed the rifle down on the wooden counter in front of her, a tiny curl of gun smoke rising from the barrel.

"Not lost your edge, I see," Nat said with a slight smile as she looked at the tightly grouped bullet holes in the target at the far end of the range. Rachel had always been the best shot of any of them, much to Jay and Jack's frustration.

"Just keeping my eye in," Rachel said. "Never know when the shooting's going to start again."

"Yeah, I suppose," Nat replied. "Though I've kind of got used to things being quieter. Can't say that I was ever a massive fan of the whole bullets and explosions side of things."

"Don't tell Jack that—he might lose interest," Rachel said, raising an eyebrow.

"I wish he would," Nat said with a laugh. They all knew that Jack had a crush on her, mainly due to the fact that he seemed to lose the power of coherent speech when she was around. Unfortunately for him it was also painfully obvious that Nat didn't feel quite the same way.

"I suppose Jay asked you to come and talk to me," Rachel said, picking up her rifle and walking toward the armory."

"He's just worried about you, you know," Nat said. "You all went through hell up there."

"We've been through worse," Rachel said. "Sam's not the first person we've lost after all."

Nat looked at her friend's face. She was right, of course. They had all experienced more than their own fair share of tragedy over the past couple of years, but that didn't change the fact that some losses were felt more acutely than others.

"I know," Nat said, "but . . ."

"Chosen of the Illuminate," the Servant said from behind them, and the two girls turned to see the golden-skinned woman walking toward them across the compound. Theoretically the former Voidborn could simply manifest anywhere she wanted out of thin air, composed as she was of a swarm of countless billions of networked nanites, but Sam had quickly made it clear that doing so made the humans around her uncomfortable.

"Please, can we just stick to Rachel," she said with a sigh. "I don't need the grand title, thanks."

"As you wish," the Servant replied. "My sensors have detected a human aircraft approaching at high speed."

"What?" Rachel snapped, frowning.

"Should I dispatch drop-ships to intercept?" the Servant asked calmly.

Rachel's mind raced. None of them had seen a non-Voidborn aircraft since the first day of the invasion.

"You're certain it's not Voidborn?" Rachel said.

"Initial sensor mapping suggests it is a twin-engined rotorcraft of rudimentary design," the Servant replied. "It is significantly less advanced than Voidborn technology."

"A helicopter?" Nat said, sounding unconvinced. "Are you sure?"

"The drop-ships would allow us to make visual confirmation," the Servant replied. "The aircraft's estimated time of arrival at the Mothership is seven minutes."

"Do it," Rachel said. She wasn't prepared to take the chance that it was some kind of Voidborn trick. "And get Stirling out here, please."

The Servant gave a nod. Moments later, far above them, the twin black triangles of two Voidborn drop-ships shot out of one of the numerous hangars that covered the upper surface of the Mothership, racing toward their target.

Mason stared out of the cockpit window of the Chinook. They were almost twenty miles from the center of London, but even at that range the vast shape of the Voidborn Mothership was clearly visible floating above the city.

"Sir," one of the pilots said, tapping the radar console between the two pilots' seats, "we have two fast movers closing on us from the direction of the Voidborn ship."

"Hold your course," Mason said calmly. "We couldn't outrun them if we wanted to. Let's see how this plays out."

A minute or so later the two triangular aircraft shot past the helicopter, one on either side. They banked back around, taking up flanking escort positions.

"Stay on this course," Mason said. "Let's not do anything to spook our new friends." The drop-ships looked identical to the ones that Mason had covertly observed flying above Edinburgh before the Voidborn Mothership had departed. The only difference that he could see was the color of the light that seemed to dance just below the crystalline surface of their skin, which glowed yellow instead of green. A few minutes later the helicopter passed into the shadow of the Mothership and Mason turned back to the passenger compartment.

"Mr. Riley, would you please join me up here," Mason said.

Sam stood up from his seat and walked between the seated soldiers and up to where Mason was standing.

"We're approaching the area that you indicated was your base of operations," Mason said. "It would appear that you might actually have been telling the truth. You'd better tell the pilot where we should put this thing down."

Sam felt a growing sense of relief as he saw the lights of the compound in St. James's Park glowing in the predawn gloom. They were back in his territory now. He directed the pilot toward the clear area in the center of the compound that was usually used as a landing site for the drop-ships. A minute or so later the helicopter hit the ground with a slight jolt and the ramp at the other end of the cabin whirred to the tarmac, the light from outside flooding into the dimly lit passenger compartment. The soldiers marched down the ramp, fanning out around the rear of the Chinook in a curved defensive line, weapons raised. Sam followed them outside and saw Jay and Rachel with their weapons raised, flanked by a pair of Grendels.

"Oh my God," Rachel said, her eyes widening as she saw Sam walk down the ramp.

"It can't be . . . Sam?" Jay said, his mouth dropping open with surprise.

"Tell your friends to lower their weapons," Mason said.

"As long as you tell your men to do the same," Sam replied.

Mason thought for a moment and then nodded.

"Stand down," Mason said to his men. The reality was that even that much concentrated firepower would do little good against the Grendels anyway.

Sam walked past the soldiers and Rachel ran toward him, wrapping him in her arms and hugging him. When after a few seconds she pulled away from him, her eyes were wet with tears. She sniffed and wiped her face with the back of her hand, staring at him as if she couldn't quite believe he was real.

"We thought you were dead," Rachel said, shaking her head in disbelief.

"If it's any consolation," Sam said with a grin, "so did I."

"I don't believe it," Jay said, grinning as he too hugged his friend. "How the hell did you survive? There were thousands of those things out there. There's no way that—"

"It's a long story," Sam said. "I'll tell you later."

"Who's that?" Rachel asked, nodding toward Mason, who was watching their reunion with interest.

"That's who we went up there to find in the first place," Sam said. "His name's Mason and he and his men have been trying to keep the Vore from spreading outside the city."

"The what?" Jay asked, looking confused.

"Sorry, that's what the creatures are called," Sam said, suddenly looking serious. "I have to speak to Stirling— he needs to know what those things really are."

"What do you mean?" Rachel asked, suddenly worried by the expression on Sam's face.

"The Vore aren't like the Hunters or the Grendels," Sam said with a frown. "That's why I couldn't sense them in Edinburgh before they attacked. They're . . . or at least they once were . . . human. The Voidborn didn't take the Sleepers with them—they turned them into the Vore."

"You mean . . ." Rachel paused for a moment. "That's obscene."

"We . . . we killed dozens of them," Jay said, feeling bewildered.

"I know," Sam said, looking down at the ground, "but what choice did we have? It was kill or be killed. They were dead long before we got there."

Sam noticed movement behind the Grendels and then Stirling appeared with William, Liz, Adam, Nat, and Jack, all looking just as stunned to see him alive.

Mason watched for a couple of minutes as Sam reunited with his friends. Stirling glanced over in his direction and nodded. He walked over to Mason and extended his hand.

"It's good to see you again, Iain," Mason said, shaking Stirling's hand. The pair of them had only met a handful of times in the decade leading up to the invasion.

"You too," Stirling replied. "I hoped that the transmission we picked up might have had something to do with you. I take it that the Faslane facility survived the invasion."

"Yes, but we weren't fully prepared," Mason replied. "I only have a fraction of the men we were supposed to be assigned. We've only recently been able to begin surface operations—we had to wait for Shaw to finish his work on these things." He tapped the implant on the side of his head.

"Daniel's with you?" Stirling said, looking confused for a moment. "How's that possible?"

"What do you mean?" Mason asked with a frown.

"He was in London on the day of the invasion," Stirling said. "How on earth did he get to you?"

"He walked," Mason said. "It took him weeks."

Stirling looked as if he was going to say something else for a moment, but then he glanced over at the children who were huddled around Sam.

"I take it you know that's his son," Stirling said.

"Yes, Daniel never really spoke about his family," Mason said. "I'd always assumed they'd been taken in the invasion. I had no idea his son was one of the implant recipients."

"He's a lot more than just that," Stirling said, raising an eyebrow.

"Yes, I've seen his arm," Mason said. "When he told me it happened while you were taking control of the London Mothership, I found it rather hard to believe. I don't know how you did it, Iain, but this could be a pivotal moment in driving back the Voidborn. If you've worked out a way to take control of a Mothership and we combine your men with mine, we could start to turn the tide."

"It's rather more complicated than that," Stirling said, looking slightly uncomfortable all of a sudden. "What exactly did Sam tell you?"

"He told me you had an army," Mason said, frowning.

"That was something of an exaggeration," Stirling replied.

"What do you mean?" Mason asked.

"That's our army," Stirling said, nodding toward the group of children who were gathered in the shadow of the hulking Voidborn machines.

"You're joking," Mason said, looking shocked. "Then how did you . . ." He glanced up at the colossal vessel hanging in the air far above them.

"Honestly," Stirling replied, "I have no idea. Besides which, it's not entirely accurate to say that *we* control the Mothership. Sam's the only one who it actually responds to. We didn't assault the Mothership—we were captured and, during the ensuing confrontation with the Voidborn consciousness inside the ship, something happened that profoundly altered it. Now it obeys the boy's instructions without question."

"How is that possible?" Mason said, looking over at the grinning boy surrounded by his friends.

"I think you should probably ask Daniel that," Stirling said. "He implanted the boy with some form of experimental nanites when his Voidborn implant started to expand uncontrollably. I've never seen anything like them before. He never told me how he developed them, but they saved the boy's life. Ever since then the Mothership has been entirely under his command. The former Voidborn that controls it calls him Illuminate, whatever that means."

Mason shook his head slightly, looking over at Sam. "I wish I could ask Shaw what he did to the boy that makes him so special," he said. "He left Faslane several weeks ago. I've not seen him since."

"Why would he do that?" Stirling asked with a frown.

"We had a disagreement on tactics," Mason said. "You need to know what's happened in Edinburgh."

"Yes, I was hoping you could give me more information about these new creatures," Stirling said.

"He calls them Vore," Mason said, glancing at Sam.

"Which is as appropriate a name as any. They're a plague, Iain, and I need your help to stop them."

Sam collapsed into one of the armchairs in the common room, profoundly glad to be back in what he now considered his home. He'd spent the last few hours filling everyone in on the details of his escape from the Vore, meeting Mag and then being rescued by Mason's men. Sam waved to Jay as he entered the room and his friend sat down in the seat opposite him, glancing at the soldiers who were sitting around checking their gear in silence at the other end of the room.

"Not exactly chatty, are they?" Jay said, jerking his head toward the new arrivals. "Don't think I've seen one of them crack a smile yet."

"I know what you mean," Sam said. "They're pretty good at the whole stone-faced warrior thing, aren't they?"

"You sure we can trust them?"

"Yeah," Sam said with a nod, "suppose so. Though it wasn't like I had a lot of say in the matter, actually. I might have just managed to survive our first encounter with the Vore, but I wouldn't have made it through the second if it hadn't been for them."

"Man, those things were grim," Jay said. "I don't want to think about what would happen if they made it to London."

"Yeah," Sam replied, "we've got to find a way of making sure that doesn't happen."

"Hey, guys," Rachel said as she sat down on the arm of Sam's chair. "Why the serious faces? Thought we were supposed to be celebrating."

"We were just talking about what the Voidborn did in Edinburgh," Sam said.

"And how we make sure they can't do the same thing here," Jay added.

"Yeah, I still can't believe that they were the city's Sleepers," Rachel said. "I thought my nightmares were bad enough already, but this . . ." She trailed off, shaking her head.

"Yep," Sam said, "the only advantage we really have is that they're nocturnal. Maybe if we move the Mothership over Edinburgh temporarily we can use the forces on board to find the nests and destroy them."

"Whatever happens, hundred of thousands of people are dead," Rachel said.

"Didn't you say that you found a whole bunch of Voidborn that had been ripped to pieces just before you met your latest girlfriend?" Jay said.

"Mag isn't my girlfriend," Sam said, rolling his eyes.

"You want to be careful," Rachel said with a grin. "You'll make Goldenboobs jealous."

"Please don't call the Servant that," Sam said with a sigh. "If it hadn't been for Mag, I would never have made it out of Edinburgh. Now you mention it, though, there's something that's been bothering me about what I found up at the castle."

"Yeah?" Jay said. "What's that?"

"How did the Vore turn on the Voidborn?" Sam said, frowning slightly. "Why create a weapon that's as dangerous to you as it is to your enemies?"

"Maybe they just lost control of them," Jay said. "You didn't see any other dead Voidborn, did you? Could've just been an accident."

"Yeah," Rachel said, "never stopped us from developing biological weapons before the Voidborn arrived, did it? I doubt the Voidborn really care about losing a few Hunters and Grendels if it means they can wipe out an entire city."

"I suppose," Sam said with a sigh. "I just hope that they didn't do it because of what happened here. If this was revenge for London . . ."

"This isn't on us," Jay said. "We just have to find a way to make sure they can never do it again."

Sam glanced over at the door as Stirling and Mason walked into the room.

"Sam," Stirling said, "Mason has asked if we would give him a tour of the compound. He's keen to see the Voidborn drilling rig. He also asked if we would show him the Mothership. I said I thought that wouldn't be a problem."

"I have to admit I've always been curious," Mason said. "I've spent most of my time avoiding the Voidborn—I wouldn't mind the opportunity to see some of their technology up close without getting vaporized."

"You okay with this?" Sam asked Stirling.

"Yes, but it's your choice, Sam," Stirling said. "It's your ship, after all."

Sam had never thought of the Mothership as belonging to him, but he supposed that it must seem a bit like that to the others.

"Okay, let's give you the guided tour," Sam said, standing up. "You two coming?"

"Nah, I'm good," Jay said. "I told Jack I'd go out on patrol with him. I'll catch you later."

"I'll come," Rachel said. "Been a while since I've been up there."

They spent the next hour or so giving Mason a tour of their own hastily constructed facilities and the bizarre Voidborn structure that loomed over the compound, which contained the dormant Voidborn tunneling machine. Then they walked back over to the Grendel that was keeping watch over Mason's helicopter.

"I need a drop-ship to transport us up to the Mothership," Sam said to the enormous creature. A moment later a golden cloud materialized in front of the Grendel, seeming to just appear from thin air. A second or two later the swarm of nanites coalesced into the familiar form of the Servant.

"So that's what the Voidborn look like," Mason said quietly to Stirling.

"Yes and no," Stirling replied. "That's the form the Voidborn chose to appear to us in when we first encountered it, when it was still hostile. The only difference was the color."

"Fascinating," Mason said, staring at the Servant as she told Sam that the drop-ship he had requested was on its way and would be there shortly. "And you're sure that the Voidborn couldn't somehow take control back from the boy."

"Honestly, I have no idea," Stirling replied. "I strongly suspect that they would have done, if it was that easy to take it back."

"That . . . or the loss of one Mothership is inconsequential to them," Mason replied.

"Yes, that possibility had occurred to me too," Stirling said.

Above them there was a deep throbbing roar as the drop-ship that Sam had requested landed next to the helicopter, its sleek alien lines making the human machine look awkward and ungainly. The hatch in the side of the drop-ship slid open and Sam followed Rachel up the boarding ramp.

"After you," Stirling said.

"Never thought I'd be climbing into one of these things voluntarily," Mason said with a grim smile as he walked inside.

Sam looked up at the giant crystalline structure at the heart of the Mothership, watching it pulse with the yellow waves of energy that powered the massive vessel. He had been here many times over the past few months, but even now his memory took him back to the first time he had seen it. Then it had pulsed with sickly green light and he had been on his way to his first true encounter with the Voidborn consciousness.

"What's the source of all this power?" Mason asked.

"The source of the ship's power is the gravity differential of the event horizon of a singularity trapped inside an artificial pocket dimension that is linked to the power distribution system via a quantum tunnel," the Servant replied.

"Sounds dangerous," Mason said, staring up at the crackling nimbus of energy that surrounded the massive black crystal at the very top of the power column.

"On the contrary," Stirling said, "it's actually remarkably safe, clean and efficient. I just wish I had the faintest idea how it works."

"Seeing as it's the only thing keeping us airborne, I'm just glad that it does work," Sam said to Rachel as the Servant led them to the top of the spiraling ramp that ran around the crystal. Like much of the Voidborn technology, the intricacies of the Mothership's design were still a mystery to them. The Servant seemed to understand the basics, but since she had lost her connection to the Voidborn she had lost access to any detailed explanation of why the Mothership worked the way it did or where the Voidborn may have originated. Sam was reasonably sure that it was all tied up somehow with his newfound status as Illuminate, whatever that meant.

The Servant raised a single hand as she approached the massive, intricately decorated black slab that barred the entrance to the Mothership's central control room. The elliptical patterns on its surface lit up with yellow light as the slab split into triangular sections and slid into the walls and floor.

The control room was quiet and the pedestal upon which the Voidborn consciousness had once rested, while in its dormant state, stood empty. Mason strode over to the windows that looked out over the abandoned city and shook his head.

"I'm still not sure I believe it even now I've seen it with my own eyes," he said. "It's exactly what we need."

"What do you mean?" Stirling asked with a frown.

"Illuminate, I am detecting another aircraft on approach," the Servant said. "It appears to be identical to the one in which you returned."

"You keep calling him that," Mason said, slowly turning toward the Servant. "He is not the Illuminate, but *I am*."

A moment later Mason's entire body seemed to flare with blue light and his appearance began to shift. His military uniform morphed into a suit of interlocking white armored panels. Seconds later an eight-foot-tall pale-skinned humanoid creature with glowing blue veins of light running back over the bald skin of its crested skull stood looming over them, looking down at their shocked faces with a sneer.

"This vessel does not belong to you, human," the creature said, pointing at Sam. "You will return control of it to me."

"Who . . . who are you?" Sam asked, his eyes wide with astonishment.

"I am Talon, last warrior of the Illuminate, and you will do as I command," the creature said, taking a single step toward Sam.

The Servant moved with impossible speed, dissolving into her cloud form and sweeping in front of Sam before re-forming in front of him, both of her hands morphing into vicious outstretched claws.

"I will not allow you to harm the Illuminate," the Servant said as behind her Sam, Rachel, and Stirling slowly backed away.

"I have no intention of harming the human," Talon replied. "In fact, I need him, for now at least. Besides, I believe he will give me control of this vessel quite voluntarily."

"Now why would I do that?" Sam asked. Behind him, several of the larger black-skinned Hunters guarding the control room rose from the pit below the Voidborn control pedestal. The energy weapons mounted in their gleaming carapaces were aimed squarely at the giant armored creature.

"Because if you don't I will release the creatures you call Vore into the city below," Talon replied, his eyes narrowing.

"Good God, the second helicopter! You're bringing those creatures into the city," Stirling said. "You can't do that—millions will die."

"A small price to pay to defeat the Voidborn," Talon replied. "You pathetic humans have no idea what is at stake. You have one minute to make your decision, boy, before the countdown on the electronic locks sealing the Vore cage expires. The only thing that can prevent it is me transmitting the disarm code. The choice is yours."

Sam's mind whirled. Who was this creature, where had he come from and what was he truly intending to do with the Mothership? Too many questions, no time for answers. Sam felt a pit open in his stomach as he had a sudden horrific vision of millions of ravenous Vore swarming through the streets below them. The creatures that Talon had transported to London would only need to reach one group of Sleepers and their numbers would begin to expand geometrically. There would be no hope of stopping them. In that instant he knew that he had no choice. Talon might be bluffing, but some gut instinct told him that this creature was more than prepared to carry through on his threat. That was not a possibility he could contemplate.

"It's okay," Sam said, putting his hand on the Servant's

shoulder before stepping in front of her and looking up at the towering armored warrior. "What do you need me to do?"

"Let me in," Talon said, raising his massive gloved hand and pressing it to the side of Sam's head. Sam felt a moment of disorientation and then he could sense Talon's presence inside his mind as the light around him faded to nothingness. It wasn't the horrific invasive feeling that he had felt when the Voidborn had entered his mind during their final confrontation. Instead he felt a sense of disembodiment, as if he were floating weightless in a black void. The voice that suddenly rang out seemed to come from all around him.

"Control cannot be taken, it must be given," the voice said. It sounded like thousands of individuals speaking in perfect, uncanny unison. "That is the way of things."

The voice sounded calm, soothing even, and yet something about it filled him with a mixture of awe and dread.

"What do I have to do?" Sam asked.

"Simply exercise your will," the voice replied. "Grant us control."

Sam thought for a moment about the idea of granting control of the massive vessel to Talon and that was it. His senses returned in a flood, the control room around him seeming impossibly bright for a moment as he collapsed to the floor unconscious.

"Excellent," Talon said with a smile, turning to the Servant. "Your services are no longer required."

The Servant gave a sudden horrible digitized shriek and her eyes flared with bright yellow light before she disintegrated, a cloud of dirty yellow dust falling to the floor where she had once stood. Rachel ran to Sam, picking his head up from the floor and cradling his limp body.

"What have you done to him?" she snapped at Talon as he looked down at them.

"The boy was overwhelmed by his union with the Illuminate," Talon said. "It is not unusual for the experience to be too much for the fragile minds of unelevated species. He will recover in time."

"If you've hurt him I'll—"

"Do what, girl?" Talon said with a sneer. "I have faced armies of Voidborn and seen civilization after civilization fall before them like grass before the scythe. What do I have to fear from one such as you?"

Stirling suddenly felt the mechanical tendrils of the Hunter behind him wrap around his arms, locking his limbs in their vice-like grip. Instinctively, he struggled for a moment, but he knew it was no use. The machine's inhuman strength was far greater than his own.

"Why are you doing this?" Stirling asked, staring at Talon. "You want to destroy the Voidborn—so do we. We can work together."

"I do not need your assistance," Talon said as another

Hunter moved toward Rachel, pulling her away from Sam's unconscious body and restraining her also, despite her fruitless struggling. Talon moved toward the central control pedestal as the final Hunter looped its black tentacles beneath Sam's armpits and hoisted his unconscious body into the air, the toes of his boots dangling just a few inches off the ground. The Hunters' skin now throbbed with a pale blue light instead of yellow, a change reflected in the patterns of light that pulsed through the walls around them.

"You will be detained for now," Talon said, and the cables that surrounded the control platform rose up and began to snake around him, slipping in between the plates of his armor and locking in place as they too began to throb with blue light. "Be thankful that you have been spared the fate of your companions below."

"What do you mean?" Stirling yelled as the Hunters dragged them from the room. "What's going to happen to them?"

"That rather depends on whether they somehow manage to escape the Vore," Talon replied.

"My God," Stirling said, "you can't mean . . ."

"I can't risk the Voidborn recapturing the drilling site once the Mothership departs," Talon replied, glancing down at the glowing display mounted in the forearm of his armor. "I released the Vore five minutes ago."

# 7

Mag glared down at the soldiers guarding the large metal container in the middle of the road beneath her. They scanned their surroundings, the bright beams of the flashlights mounted beneath the barrels of their weapons cutting through the darkness. A moment later one of the soldiers' radios crackled, the message inaudible from Mag's position. He gave a quick nod and then spoke briefly to his companion. They both jogged back down the road to the broad junction where the helicopter that had delivered the crate just a few minutes earlier waited, its rotors slowly spinning.

Mag watched them climb on board before she dropped silently to the slush-covered pavement ten feet below. She sniffed the air as she approached the crate, the stench of the Vore inside stronger than ever. She was still exhausted from the first stage of the journey. It had been two nerve-shredding and exhausting hours hanging on for dear life to the steel box as they had flown low and fast over the English countryside. Just when she had started to feel that the freezing temperatures and battering winds might prove too much for even her unnatural strength and stamina, the helicopter and its disturbing cargo had touched down at the abandoned airfield outside the city. Mag had been grateful for the few hours of rest that the break in the journey had provided, but she could not allow herself to sleep. She had to make sure that she stayed with the crate, no matter what. This second leg of the trip was much shorter as the helicopter completed its journey into London. She had leaped from the crate onto a nearby rooftop as the crate was dropped onto the street, waiting and watching as the soldiers stood guard.

"What are you doing, Mag?" she whispered to herself as she walked up to the crate. As she touched the cool metal sides of the box, a sudden insistent electronic beeping came from one end of the crate, startling her. She instinctively backed away, eyeing the box with suspicion. Without warning, the explosive bolts on the hatch sealing one end of the crate fired and the door swung downward, hitting the road with a loud metallic clang. Mag watched in horror as a Vore slowly slunk out of the box, sniffing the air. Slimy black drool trickled from its monstrous jaws as its senses were over-whelmed by the overpowering smell of the boundless quantities of sleeping prey that filled the buildings around it. Mag took a single step backward and the Vore rounded on her with a growl. Mag braced herself as the creature leaped, pivoting as it slammed into her. She gasped in pain as its claws raked her shoulder. But then using its own momentum against it, she slung it away across the street. The creature sprang back to its feet, preparing to leap again.

Mag saw a flicker of movement out of the corner of her eye as a second Vore from inside the box leaped at her. She dived to one side and the creature missed with its first pounce, sliding across the slushy street before regaining its balance and joining its pack-mate in cir-cling Mag with an angry hiss. The two creatures prowled around her, hissing and snapping their razor-filled jaws as they picked their moment to strike. She felt a moment of fear as she desperately tried to keep watching both creatures at once, feeling like a mouse being played with by a pair of cats.

Suddenly one of the creatures launched itself at her again and she drove the blade-tipped claws of her hand upward into the creature's exposed throat as it hit her, knocking her off her feet. She felt a warm gush of blood spilling over her hand as the Vore gave a gurgling howl of pain, its jaws still snapping just inches from her face despite the mortal wound she had inflicted. She pushed with all her strength, rolling the thrashing creature off her and climbing to her feet just as the second Vore slammed into her back, knocking the wind from her and pinning her face down on the ground. She tried to push herself up, but the creature's weight on her exhausted back was too great and she felt its hot, fetid breath on the back of her neck as it opened its jaws to deliver a final killing bite to its prey.

From somewhere nearby there was a sudden loud bang and the Vore's head seemed to just vanish in a black mist of blood, its limp body collapsing on top of her, now just dead weight. She rolled the creature off her back and staggered to her feet to see a boy with bright red hair walking toward her, a massive rifle shouldered and leveled straight at her.

"Wait!" Mag yelled, raising her hands in the air. "I'm not one of these things."

The boy hesitated for a moment and then there was the sudden sound of rifle fire from the other end of the street and the ground around Mag almost seemed to explode as the pair of soldiers who had been guarding the Vore just a couple of minutes before opened fire. Mag leaped behind the armored metal crate as the hail of bullets pinged off its surface. The red-haired boy ran toward her as the soldiers laid down more fire, and he threw himself down on the ground beside her. For a moment he stared at her pitch-black eyes and the jet-black veins that ran just beneath the surface of her paper-white skin.

"Sorry, don't mean to stare," the boy said after a moment. "I'm Jack. I don't suppose you know what the hell those guys at the other end of the street were doing releasing these things, do you?"

"I have no idea," Mag replied. It seemed an act of utter madness.

"Are there any others?" Jack asked, bobbing his head quickly around the corner of the crate and spotting the two soldiers advancing down the road toward them, ducking back into cover just as they opened fire again. They were pinned down.

The soldiers were only twenty yards from the crate when a puff of blood erupted from the lead man's thigh and he collapsed to the ground with a scream of pain, his rifle scattering away across the road as his hands flew to staunch the flow of blood from the fresh gunshot wound. The second soldier spun around to see Jay standing ten yards behind him with his rifle leveled at the man's chest.

"Don't," Jay said.

The soldier ignored him, swinging his own rifle up and leaving Jay with no choice. He fired just once and the soldier fell, dead before he hit the ground.

Jack jumped up from behind the crate and ran over to the other soldier, the man's blood-slick hands fumbling with the release of the holster on his hip. Just as the soldier drew the pistol, Jack slammed the butt of the sniper rifle into the side of his head, knocking him out cold.

"You okay?" Jack asked, glancing over at Jay, who was standing looking down at the dead man at his feet with a deep frown on his face.

"Yeah," Jay replied, running his hand over his head with a sigh. "Just never killed someone before." There was a world of difference between gunning down Voidborn monsters and taking another human life, even if he hadn't had a choice.

From the other end of the street they heard the sound of the idling helicopter's engines start to increase in pitch.

"Come on!" Jay yelled, turning and running headlong down the street toward the helicopter that was preparing to take off. He reached the bottom of the loading ramp and raised his rifle to his shoulder, aiming down the passenger compartment. At the far end a figure sat in shackles with a black bag over his head. Jay walked quietly toward the figure, passing by without saying anything, heading for the cockpit. He stepped inside the cramped compartment and the pilot half turned as his shadow fell over him.

"Don't move," Jay said. The pilot didn't hesitate, going for the pistol in the holster strapped to his chest. Jay swung his rifle butt, bringing it up under the man's chin, his head snapping backward as he slumped sideways in his flight seat, out cold. "No, seriously, don't move," Jay said, shaking his head.

"Jay, there's something wrong," Jack yelled, "come quick."

Jay jogged back down the compartment, past the slumped shackled figure and out onto the street. Jack was standing next to the odd-looking girl who had gone toe to toe with the Vore just a couple of minutes earlier and staring up at the Mothership. Craning his neck, Jay looked up at the massive vessel above him as the yellow lights on its surface flickered out, one by one, being replaced by glowing blue streams of energy.

"What the hell?" Jay said, as slowly the Mothership began to do something he had never seen it do before. It began to move.

"What's going on?" Jack said.

"Nothing good," Jay replied. "Sam's up there with Stirling and Rachel—they were taking Mason to see the Mothership." He couldn't be certain what was happening, but he was willing to bet that it was more than just a coincidence. "There's no way that they'd move the Mothership without letting us know first. Something's wrong—we have to get on board."

"How the hell are we going to do that?" Jack asked.

"Um, isn't that a very large helicopter behind you?" Mag said, pointing over Jay's shoulder.

"Slight problem," Jay said, looking back up the ramp leading inside the Chinook, "I just knocked the pilot out cold."

"Well, that's a bit more than a slight problem, Jay," Jack said, "since none of us can fly this thing."

"I can," a voice said from somewhere behind Jay. Jay spun around, startled. He'd assumed that the hooded figure sitting slumped against the bulkhead had been unconscious. He walked over to the prisoner and pulled the bag off his head. The man beneath the hood had a mop of curly brown hair and quick, intelligent eyes that darted from Jay's face to Jack's and then Mag's.

"You serious?" Jay asked with a frown. "Can you get us up to that thing?"

"I can get us up there," the man replied, "but whether we can do anything to stop what's happening, well, that's another question."

"What do you mean?" Jay asked with a puzzled frown.

"I rather fear that a lunatic has just taken control of that vessel," the man replied, looking Jay in the eye, "and he means to use it to defeat the Voidborn once and for all."

"That doesn't sound so bad," Jack said.

"Oh, and kill nearly every last human being on the face of the planet in the process," the man replied calmly.

"Okay," Jack said, "that *is* bad."

"How do you know all this?" Mag demanded.

"Because I used to work with him," the man replied, "until I realized the lengths he was prepared to go to achieve his goals."

"Okay," Jay said. He knew they didn't have time to sit around debating this. He had no idea how long they had before the Mothership would be out of range of the helicopter. "Where are the keys for your cuffs?"

"I think one of the guards had them," the man replied.

"Jack," Jay said, and his friend nodded and sprinted back down the loading ramp and down the street toward the fallen soldiers.

"This is Mag and I'm Jay," Jay said, quickly introducing them to the stranger, "and the guy who just went to find the keys is Jack."

"Pleased to meet you," the man replied with a nod. "My name's Shaw, Daniel Shaw."


Adam, Nat, Anne, and Liz watched as the soldiers that had been sitting in silence in the common room for most of the day suddenly gathered their equipment and filed out of the room without a single word.

"Where are *they* going?" Adam asked.

"No idea," Liz said. "They sort of give me the creeps."

"I know what you mean," Nat said, taking a sip from her mug of tea. "I've heard of the strong, silent type, but that's ridiculous."

"Guys, you have to see this," Will said, running across

the room with a panicked expression on his face. "The Mothership's leaving."

"What do you mean it's leaving?" Anne said, frowning.

"I mean, it's moving," Will said, "*away* from here. You'd better come and have a look for yourselves."

The five of them hurried outside. Above them the Mothership was moving slowly, but gathering speed, the parabolic dishes that covered its underside glowing with a blue light. On the other side of the compound the soldiers were filing on board the helicopter, whose enormous dual rotors were slowly starting to spin.

"What on earth is going on?" Will said, staring up at the giant vessel as it glided over them with a deep, almost subsonic rumble.

"Hey!" Adam shouted, running after the nearest of the soldiers. "Where are you going? What's happened to the Mothership?"

The man ignored him, never breaking step as he marched toward the helicopter. Adam put a hand on his shoulder and the soldier whirled around, delivering a vicious backhanded blow to his jaw that sent him to one knee, clutching his mouth. The soldier then turned and followed the rest of his comrades up the loading ramp and onto the helicopter. The ramp whirred shut and closed with a solid-sounding thud, and the helicopter's turbines began to roar as the pilot applied power for take-off.

"Are you okay?" Nat asked, helping Adam to his feet as they all retreated from the ferocious downdraft from the helicopter as it lifted into the sky.

"I'm fine," Adam said, looking angrily at the departing chopper. "I've got a bad feeling about this. I think we'd better get to the armory."

"Where on earth is everyone going?" Anne asked, staring up at the helicopter and the departing Mothership. "Where are the others?"

"Jack and Jay are out on patrol," Liz replied. "I have no idea where Sam and Rachel are."

"Oh God," Nat said quietly, "they went to the Mothership with Stirling and that guy Mason."

"You know that bad feeling of yours?" Will said to Adam, looking apprehensive. "I'm starting to think it might just have been spot on."

"Come on," Nat snapped, running toward the armory.

The others followed, jogging across the compound toward the heavy steel doors. Suddenly the Grendel that patrolled the compound blocked their path and roared. They froze as the giant creature gave another bellow and strode across the compound toward them, its long blade-tipped tail whipping from side to side as it flexed its knife-like claws. Its eyes glowed an unfamiliar shade of bright blue.

"RUN!" Anne screamed. Shaken from their terrified daze, they turned and sprinted away from the charging creature. Nat's first instinct was to run toward the nearest available building, but she knew that the flimsy prefabricated walls would provide little protection. She looked to her left and felt a sudden moment of hope as she spotted the looming shadow of the weird twisted building that housed the inactive Voidborn drilling platform.

"The Voidborn construct!" Nat yelled. They sprinted toward the darkened structure, looking for an opening that would lead them deeper inside, somewhere beyond the reach of the Grendel. The main entrance was sealed shut and without the Servant it would be impossible to open. Their only hope was the fact that the Voidborn had not had time to complete the building.

"Up there!" Anne yelled, pointing at a narrow gap in one of the incomplete walls. The four of them scrambled up the sloping matte-black slabs of the construct's surface, their boots fighting for purchase. Nat was the first to reach the opening, pulling herself up and over the edge with a grunt, Liz right behind her. She spun around and looked back down the wall just in time to see the Grendel reach the bottom, only a dozen yards below Adam. The massive creature slammed its claws into the blackened surface, slowly dragging itself upward, making up for its lack of agility with sheer brute strength.

"Adam, move!" Nat yelled when she saw the creature reach up toward him, missing his feet by just a yard or two. Anne and Will hauled themselves over the edge of the opening as Adam scrambled up the last few feet. He pulled himself over the edge and glanced back down at the Grendel, which was still making relentless, crunching progress up the wall.

"Go!" Adam yelled. "Get further inside! It's right beh—"

The tip of the Grendel's tail speared into Adam's back and emerged from his chest, glistening with blood. Adam made a single startled gurgling sound, his eyes wide with shock, and then the Grendel's tail flicked backward, tossing his body away through the air like a rag doll, disappearing into the darkness.

"ADAM!" Nat screamed. She took a step forward to go after him, despite every rational instinct telling her there was nothing she could do. He was gone. A moment later one of the Grendel's massive claws slammed down on the edge of the opening in a cloud of black dust. Nat staggered back toward the others who were pressed against the firmly sealed door at the far end of the narrow corridor.

There was nowhere to run.

The Grendel could not fit into the narrow gap, its outstretched claws snapping closed a few yards short of the group of panting, terrified children. It slammed into the structure, clawing at its outer surface, but the Voidborn materials were too strong. It could not batter its way in after them. A hideous black tentacle came squirming out of an opening in its wrist and slid blindly across the floor toward them. They all retreated as far back into the opening as they could, their backs pressing against the door. They watched in horror as it slid closer and closer, its sharpened tip weaving through the air just a few feet from their terrified faces.

Suddenly the tentacle froze and then withdrew, and they heard the Grendel stomp away across the compound. In the distance, Nat could hear the unmistakeable sound of a helicopter, getting louder all the time.

The Chinook raced low over the rooftops of London, heading for the resistance compound.

"We can't stay on the ground for long," Shaw said, sitting at the controls, "if we're going to have any chance of catching that thing."

Ahead of them the Mothership was now climbing away from central London.

"We need to check the others are okay," Jay said. "The compound was filled with Mason's men."

"If that's still the case, landing may not be the best idea," Shaw said, glancing at Jay.

"I know," Jay said, feeling suddenly apprehensive about what they might find. "Let's just go take a quick look-see."

He headed back into the passenger command, where

Mag was sitting on one of the long benches that ran along the bulkheads.

"Just wanted to say thanks," Jay said.

"For what?" Mag asked.

"For stopping those things from getting loose in London," Jay said.

"Your friend over there did as much as me," Mag said, glancing over at Jack, who was standing by the open hatch at the rear, watching the streets racing past beneath them. "Wasn't like I had much choice. I just happened to be there when the Vore were released."

"Maybe, but Sam told me what you did in Edinburgh," Jay said. "I know someone with guts when I see them."

"Thanks," Mag said with a crooked smile. "Though you might have actually got to see those guts first hand if you hadn't shown up when you did."

"Nice mental image," Jay said, shaking his head slightly, "thanks for that."

"We're coming up on St. James's Park," Shaw shouted from the cockpit. "I'm taking us down."

The helicopter dropped toward the abandoned compound. There was no trace of the other helicopter or the troops who'd arrived on it or, more worryingly, any of their friends. They were a few yards from the ground when Shaw saw something move out of the corner of his eye and instinctively yanked at the controls as the massive claw of the Grendel slashed toward the cockpit. The helicopter tipped backward, its rotors fighting to keep it airborne as it retreated from the hulking monster. Jack lost his footing, feeling a moment of near weightlessness before tumbling backward out of the open hatch. He hit the ground hard, feeling something snap in his shoulder as it bore the brunt of the impact. The Chinook passed by over his head as he pushed himself up on to his knees, hissing in pain at the waves of agony radiating from his shoulder. The Grendel turned back toward Jack as he scrambled awkwardly to his feet. The massive sniper rifle that had been slung over his shoulder lay between him and the advancing Grendel. At the speed at which the creature was approaching, it might as well have been on the moon.

"Hey!" Nat yelled from behind the Grendel as Will, Liz and Anne hurled the stones they were carrying at the creature. The Grendel hesitated for a moment and turned toward the other four children with a malevolent hiss.

On board the Chinook, Jay and Mag hung on for dear life as Shaw slowly brought the helicopter back under control. They scrambled to their feet as the deck beneath them steadied, and Jay ran for the heavy machine gun that was mounted to the deck, pointing out of the rear hatch.

"Turn back," Jay yelled at Shaw as he swung the long

barrel of the massive gun as far around as he could. "I need a clear shot."

Shaw yanked at the controls, trying to give Jay an angle on the monstrous creature in the compound below. The Grendel swung into Jay's field of view and he squeezed the trigger on the machine gun, the roaring noise of its fire deafening in the confined space. The massive forty-cal bullets chewed up the ground around the Grendel's feet and Jay adjusted his aim before firing again. The Grendel raised its clawed fist to protect its face as the bullets blew chunks out of its armored hide, sending thick gouts of black blood spraying through the air. With its other hand, the Grendel scooped up a massive fistful of dirt and rocks, flinging it at the helicopter and forcing Jay to take cover as the improvised projectiles exploded against the Chinook's rear hatch.

Back on the ground Jack ran to his fallen rifle. He grabbed it with his good arm and sprinted over to where the others were standing, taking up position behind Will and resting the long barrel of the massive sniper rifle on his friend's shoulder. The Grendel turned back toward them and began to advance with a roar.

"Don't move," Jack said, his left arm dangling uselessly as he pressed his eye to the high-powered optical scope mounted on top of the rifle.

"If you say so," Will said, swallowing nervously as the

Grendel stomped toward them. Jack took a deep breath and squeezed the trigger. The first shot went high, carving a furrow into the creature's armored forehead, and it increased its pace, now just twenty yards away from them, its blade-tipped tail rising into the air ready to strike.

"Jaaaaack," Will said nervously.

The rifle fired a second time, nearly deafening him. The bullet hit the Grendel in the eye and the back of the monstrous creature's head exploded. Sheer momentum kept it moving for a single pace and then its legs gave way and it slammed into the ground with an earth-shaking thud.

"Bull's-eye," Jack said under his breath with a relieved sigh.

Onboard the helicopter Jay had just managed to get back on the machine gun when he saw the Grendel fall. He watched as Jack let the rifle slide off Will's shoulder and drop to the ground, his hand going to his wounded shoulder. Jack looked up at Jay and pointed to the Mothership, shouting at him to get going. Jay knew they didn't have time to land and collect the others now—they had to get to the Mothership while they still could.

"Get us out of here," Jay yelled, hanging on to the gun, and a moment later, its turbines roaring, the helicopter lifted into the sky, heading for the Mothership.

"It's going to be tight," Shaw yelled from the cockpit

as the helicopter raced toward the Mothership.

"You think we're going to be able to find somewhere to land?" Jay asked, studying the huge black towers that covered the upper surface of the giant vessel.

"I hope so," Shaw said, glancing down at the dials in front of him, "because I don't think we've got enough fuel to land anywhere else."

"I'm starting to wish I'd stayed in Scotland," Mag said, peering apprehensively over Jay's shoulder as they crossed the outer limits of the Mothership's superstructure.

"Looks like we've got company," Shaw said as a Voidborn drop-ship shot up from beneath the helicopter.

Jay felt his stomach lurch as the Chinook plunged toward the dark canyons separating the towers.

"Get on the rear gun," Shaw said. "Try to buy us some time while I find us somewhere to land."

Jay jogged down the passenger compartment, grabbing one of the rifles from the weapons rack mounted on the wall and handing it to Mag.

"You know how to use one of these?" Jay asked.

"I know which end the bullets come out of, but that's about it," Mag said, taking the heavy weapon and eyeing it warily.

"That's a good start," Jay said with a crooked smile. "Safety's off, point it at what you want to hit and then pull the trigger. Pull it hard into your shoulder—it'll kick like a mule."

Mag nodded. Jay grabbed the handles at the rear of the heavy machine gun and swung it back and forth, looking for a target. A sizzling bolt of energy hit the corner of the loading ramp a few yards away, leaving tattered, molten metal glowing orange in the gloom. Seconds later the drop-ship appeared behind them. Jay squeezed the trigger and the machine gun roared, a stream of tracer fire arcing across the space between the two aircraft. It just missed the drop-ship. Jay adjusted his aim and fired again, the heavy rounds now striking home and blowing glowing shards off the crystalline skin of the alien ship.

The Chinook banked hard and Jay struggled to stay upright as Mag hung on for dear life to the webbing that lined the compartment. The drop-ship fired a fraction of a second too late, the crackling burst of energy going a few yards wide of its frantically weaving target. Jay fired again as the helicopter leveled out. His shots struck home, leaving more glowing scars in the surface of the drop-ship, but they didn't slow its pursuit. The drop-ship fired and this time its aim was true, hitting the cowling just below the helicopter's rear rotor. Inside the Chinook there was a massive bang and then the passenger compartment filled with thick, black, acrid smoke as warning sirens began to wail in the cockpit.

"We're losing power," Shaw yelled from the cockpit. "Strap yourselves in—we're going in hard!"

Jay and Mag strapped themselves in as the whole cabin lurched. In the cockpit Shaw wrestled hopelessly with the controls, trying to bleed off speed as the mortally wounded aircraft dropped toward the Mothership. He fought to keep them level as the altimeter bottomed out and the Chinook's landing gear slammed into the hull of the Mothership, collapsing under the weight of the impact. The massive machine tipped over, sending the shattering blades of its rotors spinning away through the air. The fuselage ground to a screeching halt, coming to rest against the side of one of the massive black towers with a crunch. Shaw released the straps of his harness and fell out with a thud. He crawled into the smoke-filled passenger compartment and found Mag helping Jay out of his harness, hanging from the wall that had just become the ceiling. The release catch finally unstuck and Mag caught Jay as he dropped out of the restraints, helping him onto his feet.

"We need to get out of here," Shaw said as Jay grabbed a rifle from the weapon rack. The compartment smelled of aviation fuel and even though they'd been running on fumes on their approach to the Mothership there was still a risk that the wrecked machine could go up in flames at any moment.

"Here," Jay said, offering another gun to Shaw, "take this."

"No," Shaw said, shaking his head. "I'm no soldier."

"Neither was I until the Voidborn arrived," Jay said, forcing the weapon into Shaw's hands. "Just take it. We have no idea what's waiting for us out there."

Shaw frowned and slung the weapon over his shoulder.

"Let's go," Mag said, peering out of the hatch at the end of the wrecked compartment. "Looks clear."

They crept out of the wreckage just as the drop-ship reappeared, racing toward them.

"Get away from the helicopter," Shaw yelled, all three of them breaking into a sprint as the ship bore down. It fired twice, the bolts of energy triggering a final explosion that knocked them off their feet. They lay still for a moment as it shot past overhead before hurrying over to the edge of a tear in the Mothership's outer skin. The long, ragged gap was filled with twisted machinery that almost seemed to be alive as the microscopic nanites that made up the entire vessel began to automatically repair the damage, new conduits weaving through the superstructure like the nervous system of some massive creature.

"There," Mag said, pointing to the dark mouth of a tunnel leading further into the gloom.

"We have no idea what's down there," Jay said, looking into the black hole apprehensively as they walked closer.

"Don't think we've got much of a choice," Mag said, the sound of the drop-ship growing louder.

"Here goes nothing," Jay said, slinging his rifle across

his back and slowly lowering himself into the hole, feeling for hand and footholds in the gently sloping tunnel. Mag followed him down. Even her enhanced senses could make out nothing in the darkness, just a faint odor of ozone floating in the air. Shaw ducked inside just as the drop-ship floated past overhead, more slowly this time, beams of light playing over the tangled smoldering wreckage of the Chinook.

After a couple of minutes Jay switched on the flashlight attached to his combat harness, lighting up the tunnel leading off into the darkness ahead. They continued along it for fifteen minutes until a glimmer of blue lit the way ahead. Jay turned off his light, creeping slowly forward with his weapon raised. As he rounded the bend, he found himself looking down into a cavernous room filled from the floor to the ceiling with columns of Voidborn Hunters, the silvery Drones suspended in shafts of bright blue light. The part of Jay that had spent so long fighting them while trying to survive on the occupied streets of London couldn't help but feel a twinge of nervousness at seeing so many of them in one place.

"They look dormant," Shaw said as he came up alongside Jay and Mag.

"Given the reception we just got from that drop-ship, I think that's probably a very good thing," Jay said. "We have to assume we've lost control of the Mothership."

"What I'd like to know is how you managed to take control of it in the first place," Shaw said, staring up at the thousands of Hunters that surrounded them.

"Well, maybe if we can get our people out of here you'll be able to ask them for yourself," Jay said. "Until then you're still in the 'don't really know, don't really trust' category."

"I can understand why you feel that way," Shaw said, "but we're going to have to work together if we're going to stop Mason."

"What's he going to do?" Mag asked.

"We isolated the location of the primary transmission node for the Voidborn control network," Shaw said. "I think he's planning to use this Mothership to destroy it."

"And leave all the Sleepers brain dead in the process," Jay said, thinking of the Sleepers who'd been severed from the Voidborn control signal in London with such disastrous consequences.

"Indeed," Shaw said. "He has to be stopped."

"Why would he do that?" Mag said, shaking her head.

"He lost everything to the Voidborn," Shaw replied. "I thought I'd seen the limits of how far he was prepared to go, but now . . ."

"Yeah, releasing the Vore in London," Jay said as they walked between the glowing columns of floating Hunters. "What on earth was he thinking?"

"And why did his men follow his orders?" Mag said. "I know that they're soldiers but . . ."

"They don't have a choice," Shaw said. "The devices attached to their skulls don't block the Voidborn control signal—they intercept and subtly alter it so that the soldiers are under his control instead. They're no more responsible for their actions than the rest of the Sleepers."

"You seem to know an awful lot about it," Jay said with a slight frown.

"I should," Shaw replied. "I designed the control devices."

"Why would you do that?" Mag asked, sounding surprised. "Why give someone like that his own private army?"

"I didn't realize at the time how dangerous he was becoming," Shaw replied. "It was only later when—"

Jay suddenly held his hand up as a Hunter floated out of one of the columns of light just ahead of them, slowly rotating as the segmented metallic tentacles dangling beneath its body twitched and writhed. The Hunter turned toward them and advanced. Jay raised his rifle, his finger curling inside the trigger guard.

"Wait," Shaw said, watching the Hunter carefully. The Voidborn creature drifted toward them and then went straight past as they parted to make way for it, eventually floating away down the tunnel from which they had just come.

"That was risky," Jay said, lowering his rifle as the Hunter disappeared from view.

"Not really," Shaw said. "I've spent long enough studying those things to know that if they're going to attack they'll do so without any hesitation whatsoever. That one didn't even seem to notice we were here."

"Can we get out of here?" Mag asked. "These things give me the creeps. The only ones I ever saw in Edinburgh were already dead, ripped to pieces by the Vore. Think I prefer them that way, to be honest."

"Yeah, I know what you mean," Jay said. They had no idea how long the Hunter's apparent lack of interest in them would last. "So how are we going to find the others?"

"Simple," Mag said, sniffing the air with a slight smile, "just follow my nose."

Rachel sat in the windowless room with Sam's head resting in her lap. His eyes slowly opened and he raised his hand to his forehead with a wince.

"Ow," he said. "What happened?"

"Whatever that Talon creature did to you knocked you out cold," Rachel said as Sam gingerly sat up, rubbing his temples.

"We've been locked in here ever since," Stirling said, gesturing at the bare, black walls that surrounded them, the only light coming from a dimly glowing panel in the ceiling.

"Don't suppose either of you have any Tylenol," Sam said.

"'Fraid not," Rachel replied with a crooked smile.

"I think we're moving," Sam said. He could feel the rumble of the Mothership's massive anti-gravity engines through the soles of his feet. The last time he'd felt that was when the

Servant had first appeared and saved the Mothership from dropping onto central London.

"It would appear so," Stirling said with a frown, "though we have no idea where we're going or why."

"There's something you need to know," Rachel said, her expression suddenly serious. "Mason released the Vore in London."

"But he said that . . ."

"I know," Rachel said with a sigh. "He did it anyway."

"Oh my God," Sam said, struggling to absorb the enormity of what Rachel had just told him. "The others, we have to . . ." He trailed off. He'd seen what had happened in Edinburgh. There would be nothing they could do. London was lost and, in all likelihood, so were the lives of his friends. "I'm going to kill him."

"It may not be quite as straightforward as that, I'm afraid," Stirling replied. "You saw his true face. I have no idea how long the man I knew as Mason has actually been this Talon creature. He clearly has access to technology far beyond our understanding; the ability to change his appearance at will is probably just a fraction of his true power. He claimed to be the last of the Illuminate and I strongly suspect that they must have been the original builders of the Motherships. If he understands the technology on board this vessel properly, and has the experience necessary to use it properly, he may prove almost impossible to stop."

"We have to try," Rachel said.

"Well, we can't do much about it from in here," Sam said, looking over at the firmly sealed door at the other end of the room. He could still sense the Mothership around him, just as he had been able to since his first encounter with the Voidborn consciousness, but his direct connection to it was severed. "Where's the Servant?"

"She's gone," Stirling said. "Talon deactivated her nanite swarm."

"So we're stuck here," Sam said, still trying to ignore the pain in his head.

"I rather fear we are," Stirling replied.

Sam sat staring at the floor for a couple of minutes, trying to make sense of what was happening.

"It's not your fault, you know," Rachel said.

"I should never have given up control of the Mothership. It didn't save anyone anyway," Sam said.

"You couldn't have known that at the time," Rachel replied, shaking her head. "None of us knew—"

She was interrupted as the door at the other end of the room hissed open to reveal one of Talon's soldiers.

"You," the soldier said, pointing at Sam, "come with me."

"Where are you taking him?" Rachel said, standing up. The soldier raised his rifle and Sam put his hand on Rachel's arm.

"It's okay, Rachel," Sam said. "I'll be fine—don't worry."

Sam raised his hands when the soldier motioned with

his gun for him to step outside. As he passed the man, he felt the same odd scratching noise inside his skull that he'd felt when he'd first been near the soldiers on the helicopter that had brought them down to London.

He glanced up at the soldier's impassive face, and the implant on the side of his skull flickered with green light. Sam suddenly realized that it was flashing in perfect unison with the scratching noise. He instinctively reached for the device with his mind, just as he had done with the Mothership's Voidborn tech. The device responded and he felt the instantaneous bond between his own mind and the alien technology as the implant inside his own skull connected to it. He sent it the quickest and simplest command he could.

*Deactivate.*

The soldier collapsed in a heap on the floor, his protection from the Voidborn control signal instantly gone. He was just another Sleeper now. Sam bent down and picked up the fallen man's rifle, throwing it to Rachel.

"You're a better shot than me," he said, pulling the soldier's pistol from the holster on his hip. "I have no idea if anyone will have noticed me doing that. We'd better get moving."

"What did you do to him?" Rachel asked, looking down at the fallen man and then back toward Sam.

"I think I found his off switch," Sam said, tapping the side of his own head.

"I still don't understand why they would help Talon," she said. "They've seen what the Vore can do—why would they willingly help him after he ordered them released in London?"

"I think there's more to those things than meets the eye," Sam said, pointing at the implant on the side of the soldier's head. "It wasn't just blocking the control signal, it was as if it was receiving another signal from somewhere else—not Voidborn, something different."

"Talon," Stirling replied. "That would make sense, I suppose. He would need to be sure that his men's loyalty was beyond question."

"Well, let's hope he's too distracted at the moment to notice that one of his puppets has just had his strings cut," Rachel said, looking both ways along the empty corridor. "Do either of you know where we are? These corridors all look the same to me."

"I tried to keep track of where we were being taken when the Hunters brought us here," Stirling said. "I think we're not far from the central hangar deck."

"Don't ask me," Sam said, pulling the spare clips for the pistol from the soldier's belt. "I just followed the Servant around whenever I was up here. It's a maze."

"We need to get to the control room," Rachel said, "if we're going to stop Talon."

"I think we're going to need more than two guns to do that," Stirling said.

"If he's prepared to release the Vore in London," Rachel said, "God only knows what he'll do with a Mothership. He clearly doesn't care how many of us have to die so he can win his war."

"Rachel's right," Sam said. "We have to do something."

"I don't disagree with you," Stirling said, "but we need a plan. We know nothing about this Talon creature or his connection to the Illuminate, whoever or whatever that is."

Suddenly, the unconscious soldier's radio crackled into life.

"Operative seven report status," the voice on the other end said.

"Let's go," Rachel said, looking nervously down the corridor. In the distance they could hear the sound of marching boots.

"This way," Stirling said, gesturing for them to follow him in the opposite direction. The three of them ran down the gently curving corridor, the sudden shouts from behind suggesting that the guards had found their unconscious companion.

"Why isn't he sending the Hunters after us?" Rachel asked as they sprinted out into the cavernous expanse of one of the Mothership's several hangar bays. All around them Hunters floated next to the drop-ships lining the floor of the bay, performing routine maintenance. None of the hovering bio-mechanical creatures paid them the slightest bit of attention—they simply continued about their appointed tasks, apparently unconcerned by the arrival of these unexpected humans.

"I have no idea," Stirling said. "I suppose we should be thankful for small mercies."

"Maybe he can't," Sam said, scanning the room for a place where they could take cover. "I never really controlled them either. I just asked the Servant and she carried out the commands herself. Maybe without her Talon can't access all of the Mothership's systems."

Sam ducked behind a large black cube that was throbbing with blue light, long glowing cables running from it to the belly of a nearby drop-ship. Rachel and Stirling joined him, crouching down, listening carefully for signs of their pursuers. It didn't take long. Half a dozen of Talon's enslaved soldiers jogged into the hangar, fanning out across the deck, weapons raised.

"We can't just stay here," Rachel whispered urgently. "They're going to find us."

Sam looked around desperately. The nearest exit from the hanger bay was fifty yards away, across the open deck. They wouldn't make it halfway before they were spotted and then they'd be sitting ducks. He popped his head around the corner of the generator and took a quick headcount of the men he could see. He didn't need to be a military genius to see that they were out-gunned. He tried to reach out and connect to their implants, but they were too far away. If he was going to pull off the same trick he'd used on the guard a few minutes earlier, he needed to get closer.

"You're going to have to make a break for it," Sam said, clicking the safety on his pistol off with his thumb and handing it to Stirling. "Don't open fire until they spot us, you'll need as much of a lead as we can get."

Rachel frowned, looking confused for a moment, her expression changing to one of shock as Sam stood up and came out from behind the generator, hands raised. It was a desperate gamble, but the only other option was for them all to give themselves up.

"I surrender," Sam said, walking toward the lead soldier, twenty yards away from him.

"The boy has been located," the soldier said into his throat mic, nodding as he received an inaudible reply in his earpiece. "Understood, proceeding with termination." The soldier raised his rifle, leveling it at Sam's head.

"No!" Rachel screamed, standing up and bringing her own weapon to bear on the advancing soldier.

Sam turned toward her, flinching when he heard the soldier's gunfire. He felt a searing pain as the soldier's bullet creased his skull, leaving a long gash in his forehead and sending him spinning to the floor. Rachel fired twice, hitting the soldier squarely in the chest, his flak jacket stopping the rounds, but the impact knocking him off his feet with a grunt. Rachel ducked back down into cover as the other soldiers opened fire, bullets pinging off the solid block of the generator and the floor around them. There was nowhere to run.

Suddenly there was a flash and the roar of automatic gunfire from the other side of the hangar. Sam saw Jay and a second figure, partially obscured by the doorway, laying down a withering field of fire that cut down one of the soldiers and forced his squad mates to run for cover. One of the retreating soldiers pointed his rifle at Sam as he forced himself to standing, blood running down over his eyes. Mag leaped from the top of the nearby drop-ship with a snarl, her claws extended and her razor-sharp teeth bared. The soldier half turned as she knocked him off his feet and pinned him to the ground, her glinting claws flashing through the air and driving deep into the man's shoulder. Her other hand bunched into a fist and she punched the soldier hard in the nose, knocking him out cold.

Sam staggered, wiping the blood from his eyes with the back of his arm as Mag threw the fallen soldier's rifle to him. He caught it as two more of the soldiers turned toward him and Mag, opening fire as they both dived for cover behind the landing skids of one of the nearby drop-ships.

"What the hell are you doing here?" Sam shouted over the thunderous sounds of gunfire that were coming from all around them.

"You mean you're not pleased to see me?" Mag said with

a grim smile as a bullet pinged off the landing gear, just inches from her head. "We can catch up later. For now I think we should probably just concentrate on getting out of here, don't you?"

"Point," Sam said, shouldering the rifle and firing a short burst at one of the soldiers who had Rachel and Stirling pinned down. They took advantage of the momentary break in gunfire and sprinted out from behind the cover of the generator toward Sam and Mag. The soldiers began a fighting retreat, pulling back toward the entrance from which they had just come.

"Come on," Mag said, gesturing for them to follow her toward the other doorway.

"Who are you?" Rachel said, looking slightly startled by Mag's appearance.

"She's a friend," Sam said. "We can trust her."

"Okay," Rachel replied, "if you say so."

The four of them made their way carefully back around the drop-ship toward the exit from the hangar. A couple of seconds later the last of the soldiers retreated from the hangar and the massive doors slid shut, closing with a solid thud.

"Looks like we've got them on the run," Mag said.

"Yeah," Sam said with a frown. The soldiers had fallen back too quickly—something was wrong.

Suddenly, Jay and Shaw sprinted out of the doorway on the other side of the hangar, turning and firing at something behind them. Sam felt a moment of dizzying bewilderment as he recognized the man running alongside Jay.

"Dad?" Sam whispered, hardly daring to believe what his own eyes were telling him.

"What?" Mag said, looking startled.

But before Sam could shout over to his father, the massive bulk of a Grendel filled the doorway behind them. It gave a bellowing roar as Jay and Shaw kept firing, their bullets little more than irritating pin pricks. A moment later, Sam felt a cold chill in the pit of his stomach as a second Grendel followed the first through the doorway, its head swinging from side to side, searching for prey.

"I fear that Talon may have rather more control over these creatures than we thought," Stirling said. He glanced up, but the worker Drones still seemed entirely unconcerned by what was happening down below them.

The Grendels stomped across the hangar deck in pursuit of Jay and Shaw. Sam and Rachel opened fire on the second Grendel, trying to attract its attention, and a few seconds later it turned toward them with a growl. Sam knew they didn't have anything with enough firepower to take out one Grendel, let alone two.

"Sam!" Jay shouted from the other side of the hangar. "Get over here—we need you!"

"You two, go head for Jay," Sam said to Mag and Stirling. "We'll cover you."

He glanced at Rachel and she gave a quick nod.

Mag and Stirling sprinted out of cover, heading for the drop-ship on the other side of the bay under which Jay was standing. At the same instant, Sam and Rachel popped up from cover and opened fire.

"Go for the eyes," Rachel yelled as they emptied the clips of their rifles into the advancing behemoth's face. The Grendel staggered, blinded for an instant, bellowing in rage. The other Grendel turned, no longer advancing on the drop-ship beneath which Jay was standing, but instead pounding across the deck toward Sam and Rachel.

"Okay, we got their attention," Rachel yelled as she tossed the empty rifle to one side. "What now?"

"Run!" Sam yelled back.

Rachel took off instantly, and Sam sprinted after her, turning just in time to see the generator spinning through the air toward him. He dived to one side as it smashed into the ground where he had been standing moments before, exploding in a shower of bright blue sparks. He climbed to his feet and again set off after Rachel, who was heading along the wall of the hangar toward Jay's position.

Sam only managed a couple of paces before he felt something incredibly strong wrap around his ankle, squeezing it tightly and yanking him off his feet. He clawed desperately at the smooth surface of the hangar deck as the tentacle protruding from the Grendel's wrist began to pull him in.

As the Grendel opened its mouth to reveal row after row of dagger-like teeth, Sam felt a moment of panic. He reached out with his implant, trying to somehow connect with the hideous creature and order it to release him, but it was useless. The Grendel was silent to him.

Just when Sam thought all was lost, a Hunter swooped across and hit the Grendel's face hard, its poison-tipped tentacles viciously stabbing at the behemoth's eyes. The startled creature recoiled, releasing its hold on Sam and clawing at the silver Drone attached to its face. Black blood oozed from the Hunter's torn shell as the Grendel's claws raked across its surface. A moment later a crackling bolt of yellow energy slammed into the Grendel's shoulder, blowing chunks out of its armored carapace as it bellowed in rage.

Sam looked up and saw a small swarm of Hunters descending from the ceiling, the glittering surfaces of their shells glowing with yellow light. They fired at the Grendels, spitting bright yellow energy bolts. Other Hunters swooped down, their barbed tentacles seeking the holes that had been torn in the armor and snaking inside. The Grendels flailed uselessly, quickly succumbing to the tide of energy blasts and stabbing tentacles. Sam didn't stop to think about what was happening—he just sprinted across the hangar toward the drop-ship that Jay was frantically beckoning him toward.

"You need to get on board," Jay yelled as Sam

approached. "Shaw needs you to help him get this thing moving."

Sam didn't have time to tell Jay who Shaw was; he just nodded and ran up the ramp. Inside the others were waiting, their faces a mixture of confusion and fear. At the other end of the drop-ship Stirling was standing talking quickly and quietly to a man who had his back turned to them. Sam felt his heart jump as Stirling glanced over the man's shoulder at Sam and the man turned around.

"Sam," Shaw said, "thank God you're okay. I know I have a lot to explain, but there's no time. I'll answer all your questions when we've gotten out of here, but now I need your help."

Sam stared back at the man whom he had thought he might never see again, his father. His mind was filled with a thousand questions, but the expression on his father's face told him that they would indeed have to wait.

"What do you need me to do?" Sam asked.

"Help me fly this thing," Shaw said, walking toward Sam and placing his hand on the side of his head. Sam felt a moment of confusion and then he heard his father's voice inside his head.

*Don't panic, just let me in.*

A moment later the drop-ship lifted from the ground with a lurch, its startled passengers fighting to keep their balance as it turned and powered across the hangar, heading for the glowing force field at the far end and the open sky beyond. The black triangular aircraft shot through the glittering field and out into the pre-dawn sky, the throbbing roar of its engines increasing as it was pushed to the very limits of its performance envelope.

On board the drop-ship Shaw closed his eyes and the aircraft dived toward the ocean, thousands of yards below them. They flew along in silence for a couple of minutes, Shaw kneeling next to Sam, his hand still pressed to his son's head, his eyes closed.

"Thank you," Shaw said, finally opening his eyes and smiling at Sam and lowering his hand from the side of his son's head.

"For what?" Sam asked, his senses returning in a bewildering rush.

"For trusting me," Shaw replied. "We should be beyond their reach now."

"How did you do that?" Sam asked. "How did you know how to fly this thing?"

"I can explain," Shaw said. "There's—"

Shaw suddenly felt something cold and hard press against the back of his skull.

"Who are you?" Stirling demanded, pressing the muzzle of his pistol into the back of Shaw's head and cocking the hammer.

"Iain, it's me, Daniel," Shaw replied.

"Doctor Stirling, what are you doing?" Sam asked, his

own look of bewilderment matching the expressions of the others in the cabin.

"I know Daniel Shaw—we were friends and colleagues for years," Stirling said, scowling. "Whoever you are, you're not him."

"Iain, I have no idea what you're talking about," Shaw said, raising his hands.

"If you were Daniel Shaw, you'd be fast asleep in a building somewhere in London right now," Stirling said, "because the Voidborn implant that would have protected you from the control signal is inside Sam's head, not yours. You have no protection from the signal, so how come you're standing here in front of me? I knew something was wrong when Mason told me that you had arrived in Edinburgh, but now maybe you can explain to me in person why you suddenly seem to be inexplicably immune to the Voidborn control signal."

Sam suddenly realized that what Stirling was saying was true. The device in his own head had been the first of its kind when it had been surgically implanted, but it had been reverse engineered from the implant the Voidborn had given his father when he was working for the Foundation. His father should have been just as vulnerable to the control signal as anyone else.

"Iain, please, I really can explain," Shaw said. "You don't need the gun."

"I'll be the judge of that," Stirling replied. "Now, tell me who you are and what you're doing here."

"I am Daniel Shaw," he replied, "and I was Andrew Riley, but before that . . ."

He paused for a moment and looked at Sam with a sad smile. A moment later his entire body flared with blue light and Stirling stepped backward with a gasp. Shaw grew in stature before their eyes, his shirt and jeans vanishing, replaced by loose-fitting white robes as he looked down with new eyes at Sam's startled face. The thick mop of brown curly hair was gone, replaced by a pattern of blue lights that danced across the pale skin covering the creature's crested skull.

"Before that," the creature said, its voice now deeper, "I was Suran, last Sensate of the Illuminate."

He looked down with a sad expression at the startled faces of the humans facing him, his eyes seeming to speak of a thousand witnessed horrors.

"And I need your help."

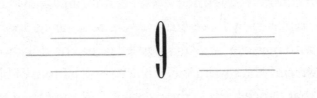

9

"No, that can't be true," Sam said, backing away from the eight-foot-tall creature standing in front of him. "What have you done with my dad?"

"I am your father, Sam," Suran replied. "I am Andrew Riley; I am Daniel Shaw. To the Illuminate, the physical form is meaningless—what matters is the consciousness within. All else is subject to change." He stepped toward Sam, raising a hand.

"Stop," Stirling snapped. "If you take one more step, I'll kill you where you stand."

"No, you won't," Suran said, turning back toward Stirling. "You're still the man I knew for all those years, Iain. You're no killer."

"He may not be, but I am," Jay said, raising his rifle.

"Do I really need to remind you who is piloting the assault

vessel traveling at hyper-sonic speeds, within which you are currently standing?" Suran said, turning toward Jay with a frown. "And was I not the one who piloted that primitive machine that brought us on board the colony ship? Why would I have done that or assisted you in finding your friends if I wished you harm?"

"Maybe you just wanted to hook back up with your partner," Rachel said.

"Partner?" Jay asked.

"Yeah, that guy Mason turned out to be another of 'the last' of these things," Rachel said. "He called himself Talon. He released the Vore on London."

"Actually, that might not have quite panned out the way he was expecting it to," Mag said, still staring wide-eyed at Suran.

"Yeah, we took care of the Vore," Jay said. "London's safe. Thanks to Mag and Jack."

"Oh thank God," Rachel said. "What about the others?"

"They're still in London," Jay said. "Jack stayed with them. They're safe—for now, at least."

"It is true," Suran said, looking down at the floor. "Talon is the last of our warriors, just as I am the last of our Sensate. I am what humans would call a scientist. What he is doing, what he has done already, sickens me to my very core. The light has gone from him. He has lost his mind to grief."

"Why are you here?" Stirling said, lowering the pistol.

"If what you say is true, why have you been hiding among us for all this time?"

"To understand that you must first understand the Voidborn," Suran replied. "If anyone truly can."

"And you do understand them, I suppose?" Stirling said.

"Yes, I do," Suran replied, "because I fear I may have inadvertently helped to bring them to your planet."

"You did what?" Sam said, sounding horrified.

"Please, let me explain," Suran said. "My people were vastly more technologically advanced than your species. We had long been explorers, just like the human race, but we had reached the boundaries of the possible. Your Einstein was right: if there is a means of super-luminal travel our finest scientists could not discover it."

"Super what?" Mag asked.

"Super-luminal, meaning faster than the speed of light," Suran replied. "We realized that the only way we would ever be able to explore the far corners of our galaxy and beyond would be if we could divorce ourselves from mortality. Time is the great enemy to interstellar exploration. No living being could conceive of a journey that might last tens or even hundreds of thousands of years. Only machines have the infinite patience for that, but what good is it to send a machine on such a mission when the civilization that dispatched it might be ruins and dust by the time it reaches its destination?

It had long been a conundrum that even our greatest minds could not solve; indeed many thought we would forever be trapped within our own little corner of the cosmos."

"So what changed?" Sam asked, still struggling to believe that the creature who stood before him might actually once have been his father.

"We achieved immortality," Suran said, "and it changed everything. It was one of the greatest scientific endeavours we had ever undertaken, to digitize the consciousness, to record and store the electrical activity within an individual's brain."

"The scanning technology and storage requirements would be inconceivable," Stirling said, shaking his head. "How would you even know if what you recorded was actually you at all?"

"A philosophical question that my people spent many years debating," Suran said, "but to the average person it was actually quite straightforward. There was no break in consciousness, one was simply transferred instantly and completely to the Illuminate, a waking dream where time was meaningless and the only limitations to what you could do or experience was your own imagination. But first our society fought a long and bloody civil war over the technology that lay at the heart of the process. After the war, it was decided that this technology would be entirely forbidden. The dream of immortality seemed lost, rigidly controlled by a society that feared its consequences."

"You sound as if you didn't approve," Stirling said.

"Indeed, I did not," Suran replied with a frown. "I was—I still am—a man of science. The idea that my people would continue to strip their own home system of resources as their numbers increased geometrically had only one possible end point. Unless we found a way to expand outward beyond the stars we were doomed to extinction. Limited resources and an ever-expanding population can, after all, only end one way. So I spearheaded a project to create the first interstellar mission, a project that could only ever work if the vessel in question was controlled by a digitized consciousness. A ten-thousand-year journey is not so terrible when you can be stored in a perfect dreamless sleep for the vast majority of it. For that to be possible we had to persuade our leaders that in this one limited instance we should use the digitizing process to create our pilot. Finally we were granted permission and we chose our subject, a brilliant scientist. The vessel in question was called the Primary Architect, or Primarch as it came to be known, and its mission was to travel to another nearby star system and assess its suitability for colonization. If it discovered a suitable system, it would begin construction of the facilities required for habitation before signaling that the system was ready for colonization. When the Primarch was launched, we knew that some of us might not live to see it complete its mission, but it was the first small yet essential step in interstellar travel. A lone Illuminate mind crossing the gulf of space and preparing the way for the rest of us."

"And that was how you encountered the Voidborn?" Sam asked.

"No, that was later," Suran said. "You see, something went wrong. We lost contact with the Primarch only two years into its journey. It was, for a long time, the worst day of my life. The scientist whose consciousness had been digitized, the pilot, was a dear friend of mine and his loss was hard to bear. The hardest part was not really knowing what had happened to him and, rightly or wrongly, I blamed myself for his loss.

"Over the next two decades things went from bad to worse for my people. There were simply too many of us and our society was being torn apart by plagues and constant war. It was against this backdrop that our people finally decided to allow the widespread use of consciousness digitization. In the years since the civil war we had made useful advances in the technology required for the process, but more significant were the advances we had made in nano-technology. We had perfected the means to create machines that were infinitely flexible, adapting their form and function to whatever task was required of them. When coupled with the digitization of our consciousnesses, it meant we could live as electronic versions of ourselves for the vast majority of the time and then construct bodies for ourselves when we needed to interact with the physical world. At first the forms we could assume were rudimentary, but in time they became more sophisticated."

He held his hand up in front of him and it momentarily disintegrated into a swirling cloud of dust before solidifying again into its original shape.

"The irony was of course that once connected to the Illuminate, as the network that stored our consciousnesses was called, most of my people lost all interest in the physical or 'real' world, instead choosing to spend their entire lives immersed in this new reality. For some of us, though, now we were truly freed from the bonds of our mortality, the stars still beckoned. We traveled across the galaxy, the speed of our vessels now irrelevant; a journey that lasts ten thousand years is the same as one that takes a second if you are not aware of the time passing."

"What about the people you left behind?" Rachel asked. "Did you not have anyone you loved? Anyone who cared you were gone?"

"For a mortal who is still bound by the restrictions of organic life, it is perhaps hard to understand what the Illuminate became. Many individuals merged into collective consciousnesses, sharing all thoughts and experience."

"That sounds horrific," Stirling said, his brow furrowed.

"From your current perspective, yes, I suppose it does," Suran replied, "and, as it happens, I agree. For some, it was less of a concern. Traditional notions of family and loved ones ceased to be relevant for many of my people. Our society changed irrevocably: our concept of time, our understanding of our place in the real universe and perhaps most dangerously of all our sense of our own vulnerability. Our home planet was struck by a gamma ray that burst from a hypernova in a nearby star cluster. It was utterly devastating and many billions of digital consciousnesses were irretrievably erased. We thought we had protected ourselves by distributing the data storage sites for the Illuminate across the planet, but we had never considered that the planet itself could be so devastated in an instant. If we were to ever avoid a repeat of such a disaster, we needed to distribute the Illuminate across the universe. So that was exactly what we did. We sent our colony ships across the galaxy and they built a vast web of networked storage sites on countless worlds, and like fools we thought ourselves truly safe once more. Then, one day, a colony ship reported that it had found the Primarch in orbit around a world nine thousand light-years away from the point where we'd lost contact. I was amazed but also excited, because it was entirely possible that my friend's consciousness had survived, encoded within the ancient vessel."

"Hold on," Sam said, "you said that your people never worked out how to travel faster than the speed of light. How had the colony ship that found it managed to travel just as far?"

"Because we found the Primarch seventeen thousand years after it was launched," Suran replied.

"You've lived for seventeen thousand years?" Sam said, his eyes wide with astonishment.

"A little bit longer actually," Suran replied, "though I've only been truly conscious for a tiny fraction of that time. I had thought the Primarch lost forever and I was stunned that we had found it, but then something odd happened. We lost contact with the colony vessel. More ships were sent to investigate, but we lost contact with them too. The consciousnesses stored on board those vessels were safely backed up within the Illuminate network so there was no real harm done, but still it was a mystery. Very shortly after that we had our first encounter with the Voidborn. One of our ships reported coming under attack by unknown forces that were using one of our own colony vessels and then we lost contact, the consciousnesses piloting our vessel were gone, erased without trace.

"Barely a year later our home system was attacked. The Voidborn created a singularity, what you would call a black hole, in the center of our system, destroying every shred of our home worlds in the space of a few hours. It was catastrophic, but not the disaster it might have been if we had not already spent thousands of years distributing the Illuminate across the stars. We had no idea who the Voidborn were, only that they were using our own technology against us and were utterly malevolent. We were not warriors, though we were soon forced to become so."

"And you think the Voidborn had something to do with this lost vessel, the Primarch?" Sam asked.

"We still do not know," Suran said. "There have been countless rumors of something beyond the Voidborn, something that controls their actions, but no hard evidence. We found ourselves in full retreat, fleeing from Illuminate node to Illuminate node, with no battle plan to speak of. Talon was the last of our commanders and he fought like I have never seen any other fight to stop them, but trillions of Illuminate consciousnesses were lost forever. We made a last stand at the final active node, knowing that if we fell we would lose not just the battle but also the last remaining Illuminate consciousnesses.

"The Voidborn attacked with such numbers that we knew they must have thrown their entire fleet at the last node and I am ashamed to say that in our desperation we sank to their level. We created an artificial super-massive black hole and in the process destroyed a galaxy in trying to stop them, three hundred billion stars, blinking out one by one. It is the single most horrific thing I have ever witnessed. We managed to destroy all but a tiny remnant of the Voidborn fleet, but still we were forced to flee before them, trying to find a hiding place for the last remnant of our people.

"Our fastest ship made a desperate run to one of the remotest corners of known space carrying the Heart, a final compressed archive of the Illuminate as it had been before the Voidborn. The consciousnesses stored within the Heart are dormant, compressed as far as they can possibly be and stored within a near indestructible crystalline matrix. It is the last trace of our people and it is concealed from the Voidborn, we hoped forever, floating within the molten iron core of a small blue planet in the third orbit of its rather humble star. We buried the Heart and then we slept, dormant, deep beneath the surface of the planet, waiting and hoping for a time when the Voidborn were gone and we could emerge from our long hibernation and reclaim the stars."

"My God," Stirling said, "that's why they're here. They're not interested in Earth, just what's hidden inside it."

"Yes, it would appear so," Suran said with a nod. "When we arrived, there was no intelligent life on Earth—it was the perfect hiding place—but somehow they found us."

"How long ago was this?" Sam asked, feeling slightly dizzy at what Suran had just told them.

"Around five hundred million years ago," Suran

replied. "We were only awoken from our long sleep when Voidborn transmissions were picked up by our vessel's sensors. That was twenty-five years ago. I fear we may have slept too long."

"The Voidborn have been manipulating humanity for thousands of years, though," Stirling said. "Why did it take so long for you to realize?"

"The Voidborn may be utterly malevolent, but they are not stupid," Suran replied. "They acted with enough subtlety on your world that we did not detect their presence until it was too late."

"Why haven't they just destroyed the planet?" Jay asked. "From what you've said, that wouldn't have been much of a problem for them."

"We don't know," Suran replied. "Before now they've been utterly without mercy. They've never gone to such lengths to preserve life as they have done here, nor have they spent so long apparently meticulously planning their invasion. It is as much a mystery to me as it is to you, I'm afraid."

"So, where do we go from here?" Sam said.

"We have to beat Talon to his target," Suran replied. "The existence of your race is now also at risk."

"What is he planning to do?" Rachel asked, sitting down on the floor and resting her back against the drop-ship's crystalline wall. She looked exhausted— they all did.

"I believe he's going to destroy the primary Voidborn control node, which will in turn bring down the entire Voidborn fleet that is currently scattered across the planet," Suran replied. "That will also cut off the control signal to the sleeping masses of humanity. As I'm sure you're already aware, the consequences of that would be catastrophic."

"Why?" Mag asked, looking confused. "Isn't that exactly what we want?"

"No, breaking the Voidborn's control over humanity is more complicated than that," Stirling said. "Our own experiments with jamming the signal have left the subjects with irreparable brain damage."

"So we just go on allowing the Voidborn to turn people into monsters," Jay snapped. "What happens when they release the Vore somewhere else? They've already taken one city—people are going to die either way."

"The Voidborn did not create the Vore," Suran said, staring at the floor, his head bowed. "I did."

"You did *what?*" Sam said, feeling suddenly sick to his stomach.

"You mean it was you?" Mag said, pointing at her own face. "You did this to me."

"It was an accident," Suran said. "I was experimenting with integrating Illuminate nanites into the human central nervous system, an extension of what the implants inside your heads are doing right now. The theory was it

would provide anyone who was exposed to the nanites with a natural resistance to the control signal. What I didn't know was that there was something already inside the test subjects we retrieved from Glasgow, some form of Voidborn technology that we had not seen before. The nearest comparison I can think of is a computer virus, some form of their own nano-technology that interacted in a completely unexpected way with our own. Instead of freeing the subjects from the Voidborn, it transformed them into the Vore. Even worse than that, the creatures clearly had the ability to spread the nanites via their bite, spreading the infection to any human they encountered."

"Which explains why Talon only brought a couple of them to London," Rachel said. "That was more than enough to create a whole army of the things."

"Exactly," Suran said with a nod. "When I realized what we had created, I was horrified and I immediately ceased all experimentation, but Talon, well, he saw it differently. He saw a means to turn the Voidborn's slaves against the Voidborn and to drive them away from the drilling sites they had set up. He released the creatures in Edinburgh and the Voidborn were forced from the city in days. When I discovered what he had done, I realized that any trace of the Illuminate I had once known in him was gone. He had to be stopped. I tried to kill him, but he froze me in my human shape in such a way that only he or another member of the Illuminate could free me. We call it form-lock. It was a process used to imprison those who had broken our laws or who were deemed a threat to society. It returned our mortality, locking us in a physical form that was vulnerable and therefore more easily controllable."

"Hard to lock up a cloud of vapor," Jay said, raising an eyebrow.

"Indeed, but what Talon did not know was that he and I were not the only remnants of our species on the Earth. I had used Illuminate nanites to save Sam when the Voidborn implant in his head began to grow uncontrollably. I believe that is why he was able to take control of the Voidborn Mothership and help me to reverse my own form-lock. The union of Voidborn and Illuminate technology within Sam has allowed him to become an interface through which we can take control of the Voidborn. It allowed me to take control of this assault craft, just as it allowed Talon to take over the Mothership." He turned toward Sam. "I did what I did in order to save your life, but I fear that in the process I may have transformed you into a target. For that, I am truly sorry."

Sam looked down at his own golden hand and suddenly he realized that he was never going to be quite human ever again. He was one of the last relics of a war that had lasted millions of years and that might just destroy everything and everyone he had ever known before it had run its course.

"Where is this central control node?" Sam asked, trying to keep the rising anger he felt from his voice.

"Tokyo," Suran replied, "we should arrive within two hours."

"Tokyo?" Jay said. "You're kidding, right?"

"No, it is a site of particular tectonic instability, which actually suits the Voidborn's purposes well," Suran replied. "I triangulated the position of the primary control node months ago—it was not difficult, given what we knew about the Voidborn command network. The Motherships, are, after all, merely Illuminate colony ships that have been transformed to serve the Voidborn. We knew where the primary node was—we just didn't know how to get to it without a Mothership of our own, or how to deactivate it without killing all humans under the signal's control. I now realize that must have been Talon's plan all along."

"Do you think he's going to release the Vore on Tokyo?" Jay asked.

"He doesn't need to," Suran said. "He has a Mothership, or at least partial control of one, and that is all the power he will need. I do not believe he expects to survive the attack. This is a suicide run."

"What do you mean by partial control?" Stirling asked.

"As I explained, with Sam's help I was able to subvert

his control of this vessel," Suran replied. He gestured at the walls surrounding them. "I believe that Talon may be unable to control an entire ship. The colony vessels were never designed to be controlled by anything other than an artificial intelligence. One mind, even an Illuminate mind, would find the mental strain of controlling an entire Mothership overwhelming."

"Which is why the Hunters attacked the Grendels in the hangar," Sam said, "though I wasn't aware of telling them to do it."

"They would have defaulted to their most basic pre-programmed behaviors if they were not under direct control," Suran said. "Primary among those is the directive to protect all Illuminate life from harm."

"And you were just weird enough to qualify," Jay said, raising an eyebrow at Sam.

"Not complaining," Sam said with a sigh. "If it hadn't been for them, I'd be dead."

"So, what do we do when we arrive in Tokyo?" Stirling asked. "I can't really see the Voidborn welcoming us with open arms."

"I believe that I can mask our presence from their sensors," Suran replied. "To them we will look like just another one of their own assault vessels. The illusion will not be complete, but it should be enough to get us close."

"Then what?" Rachel asked.

"I have no plan for this eventuality," Suran said.

"Looks like we're going to be making it up as we go along again," Jay said.

"Yeah, because that's always worked so well in the past," Rachel said with a sigh.

"We'll come up with something," Sam said. "We always do."

"There you go," Rachel said, applying a small dressing to the wound on Sam's forehead. She handed the first-aid kit to Jay, who slipped it back into his pack. "So that's the girl who saved your backside in Edinburgh, then."

"Yeah," Sam said, glancing over at Mag, who was curled up with her hands around her knees in a corner of the dropship's passenger compartment. "You should go and say hello. She doesn't bite. Well, actually she does, but I think she's on our side."

"Yeah, probably should introduce myself properly," Rachel said, standing up and walking over to where Mag was sitting.

"Hi, I'm Rachel," she said, sitting down next to Mag. "Just wanted to say thanks for the help earlier."

"I'm Mag," the other girl replied with a nod. "I did what I did to help Sam, not because I want to be part of your little group. I think I'd have trouble fitting in, looking like this."

"Yeah, you're probably right," Rachel said with a crooked smile. "What with the human-alien hybrid, golden robot, and collection of teenagers with mind-control jammers implanted in their heads, I'm not sure we'd ever be able to find room for someone as weird as you."

"I can see why he likes you," Mag said after a few seconds, looking at Rachel.

"Who?"

"Sam," Mag said. "When I first met him, he told me all about you and how you'd saved his life when you first met. He thinks a lot of you, you know."

"Yeah, I feel the same," Rachel said, looking over at Sam, who was on the other side of the room talking to Jay. "We've all had a lot to process since the Voidborn arrived, but Sam's had more to deal with than anyone else and he still keeps going. When we thought he was dead and I found out that he'd transferred control of the Mothership to me and not Stirling . . . well . . . let's just say that it gave me a slightly better understanding of how much responsibility he's carrying around the whole time. He just never shows it."

"I guess we all do what we have to do," Mag said. "He's got a good heart. It's not everyone who could see past the way I look, but it was like it didn't matter to him at all. He saw me, not the monster."

"You're not a monster," Rachel said. "I should

know—I've met a few and, trust me, you'll know one when you see one."

"Maybe, but I'm not going to be asked to do children's birthday parties either," Mag said with a grim smile. "That's why I came after him and Mason. I knew something was wrong about that man and I didn't want Sam walking into a trap alone."

"Well, I'm very glad you did," Rachel said, "because, from what Jay tells me, if you hadn't, London would be on its way to being overrun by the Vore right now. You might just have saved millions of lives, you know."

"At the time I was more focused on saving my own skin, to be honest," Mag replied.

"Yeah, well, that's how it goes most of the time," Rachel said with a chuckle, "at least in my experience."

On the other side of the compartment Jay glanced over at the two girls chatting.

"Can you imagine what it must have been like for her?" Jay said to Sam, leaning his head back against the compartment bulkhead. "It was hard enough living through the invasion, but can you imagine what it must have been like waking up in a city filled with Vore and finding yourself . . . *changed* like that?"

"I know," Sam said. "Doesn't really bear thinking about. It's like I told you before, I'd never have made it out of Edinburgh without her."

"You okay?" Jay asked quietly, looking at his friend with a slight frown.

"What do you mean?"

"I mean about your dad." Jay glanced at the doorway to the forward compartment where Suran and Stirling had been talking quietly for the past few minutes.

"That's not my dad," Sam said, shaking his head. "He's just the thing that was pretending to be him."

"I don't think you mean that," Jay said.

"How do you know what I mean?" Sam replied, irritated.

"Hey, chill. I'm just saying that if we're really just about to go up against this Talon guy, maybe you want to talk to him now. You might not get the chance later, you know."

"I wouldn't know where to start," Sam said, staring at the floor. "I just can't shake this feeling that my whole life has been a lie and he knew all along and kept the truth from me."

"So go and get the truth now," Jay said, "while you still can."

Sam stared at Jay for a moment and then stood up with a sigh. "Okay, you're right." He looked over at the doorway.

"Aren't I always?" Jay said with a grin.

Sam walked into the forward section where Suran and Stirling were engaged in hushed conversation. Stirling glanced up at Sam as he approached.

"I'll leave you two alone," Stirling said. "I should imagine you have much to discuss."

Sam watched as Stirling left the room, turning back to Suran just as the alien creature shifted into his human form.

"Hello, Sam," his dad said. "I suppose you don't like me very much right now."

"Please don't use that face," Sam said, frowning. "It was just a mask all along."

"You're wrong," his dad replied. "I used this form to infiltrate the Foundation, but it became far more than just an assumed identity to me. I spent years in this body, I fell in love with your mother in this body and then I fell in love with you and your sister. It may not have been the life I was born to, but it came to mean just as much to me nevertheless. I'm not fighting the Voidborn to save the Illuminate anymore—I'm fighting them to save humanity. This is my home now."

"Maybe that's all true," Sam said, "but you've been lying to me my whole life. You can't expect me just to forget that. Please, change back."

Sam's father stared at him for a moment and then shifted into his Illuminate form.

"I never intended to hurt you," Suran said. "You have to understand that my people are gone. We may never retrieve the Heart, at least not before the Voidborn have destroyed it and, even if we do, we no longer have the technology to awaken them again. It could take centuries for the Illuminate to return to what it once was and maybe even then it never should. You, your sister, and your mother were my *new* life. Everything I did, I did to protect you, not to reawaken the ghosts of my former home world."

"Oh, come on," Sam said angrily. "I was just a test subject to you. A baby that you could implant with unproven, probably dangerous technology. You didn't care about me."

"I cared for you as much as any father cares for his child," Suran replied. "We had already adopted your sister. Your mother always wanted children, but I told her that it wasn't possible. I didn't tell her that it was because we were not even the same species. That would probably have been unwise."

"So, she never knew," Sam said.

"No, there was no reason for her to know," Suran said. "What good would it have done?"

"It would have been the truth," Sam said, "something you're not very comfortable with, apparently."

"Sam, I know this is hard for you," Suran replied, "but I need your help if we're going to have any chance of stopping the Voidborn and Talon. This war has already claimed countless trillions of lives. I will not allow it to claim billions more innocent victims. They have to be stopped, and for that I need you to trust me."

"That's a big ask," Sam said, staring at the alien features of the creature in front of him, searching for any trace of the man he had once known. "Do you have a plan?"

"Actually, I think I do," Suran replied. "Though it is dangerous and there is something that I must teach you first. Give me your hand."

Sam offered his human hand to Suran.

"No, the other one," Suran replied.

Sam held out his golden metallic hand and Suran took it in his own. Suran closed his eyes and a moment later the golden surface turned into perfectly normal human skin.

"There is much you need to know about your heritage and your abilities," Suran said, "and I fear I do not have the time to teach you properly. It would be far easier, if you would allow it, if I simply *gave* you the knowledge."

Sam looked at Suran for a moment and then nodded. Suran reached up and placed his hand on the side of Sam's head and closed his eyes.

A few minutes later Sam walked out of the forward compartment with Suran following just behind him.

"Okay, listen up, everyone," Sam said as all the heads in the room turned in his direction, "here's what we're going to do."

The drop-ship swooped low over the Tokyo skyline, banking toward the unmistakable shape of the Voidborn Mothership that hovered over the center of the city. Suran looked at the image of the city hanging in the air in the forward compartment of the drop-ship, studying the giant vessel and the swarm of other Voidborn-controlled aircraft.

"They are greater in number than I had anticipated," he said with a frown.

"Shouldn't make any difference," Sam said, trying to sound as confident as he had when he had outlined their plan to the others. "In fact, it may even help."

"How close can we get before they detect us?" Stirling asked.

"If we do nothing to draw undue attention to ourselves, then we should be able to get close enough for our purposes," Suran replied. "Superficially, we will appear to them to be just another assault vessel. If they conduct a thorough scan of the vessel, however, its origin will quickly become obvious."

"Maybe they'll just think that their London cousins are popping over for a visit," Jay said.

"If they do detect us, we will be vaporized within seconds," Suran replied, not taking his eyes off the display.

"Okay, not a fan of lightening the mood," Jay mumbled, rolling his eyes.

"We are five minutes from our target destination," Suran said. "I suggest you make final preparations."

"Come on," Sam said, leading Jay back into the rear compartment where Rachel and Mag were looking down at the weapons spread on the floor.

"Two rifles, magazines half empty," Rachel said,

gesturing at the guns at her feet, "and one pistol, also with only half a clip. Not exactly a kick-ass arsenal."

"It doesn't matter," Sam said, shaking his head. "If everything goes according to plan, we won't need them."

"If everything doesn't go to plan, it's not as if we're going to be shooting our way out anyway, let's face it," Jay said, running his hand nervously through his dreadlocks.

"Let's just hope it doesn't come to that," Sam said.

In the forward compartment something on the view screen caught Stirling's attention.

"What on earth is that?" he said, pointing at the display.

"That, unless I am very much mistaken, is the primary node for the Voidborn control signal," Suran replied. The image on the screen showed the building that had once been the Tokyo Skytree. The six-hundred-yard-tall spire still dominated the skyline of the city, but now its surface was covered in strange black cuboid outcroppings that twinkled with coronas of green light. Pulsing energy cables ran between the huge black blocks, entwined within the tower's white tubular steel framework, making the massive structure look almost alive. From its peak a bright red crackling stream of energy shot into the sky, vanishing into the clouds above.

"So that will be Talon's primary target," Stirling said.

"Presumably, yes," Suran replied with a nod.

"How long before he arrives?" Stirling asked.

"It's hard to say," Suran replied. "The colony ships are

not well suited to atmospheric flight . . . It could be several hours."

"More than enough time," Stirling said with a nod. "You're certain that we can't use that thing to wake the Sleepers?"

"My research would suggest otherwise, Iain, as I suspect yours did too," Suran replied.

"Indeed," Stirling said, "but it is frustrating to be so close to the root cause of our domination and not be able to do something about it. We just have to protect the node from Talon's assault. It almost feels like we're helping the Voidborn."

"We are protecting humanity, so that perhaps we can wake them in the future. You know as well as I do that we should not wake all the enslaved simultaneously anyway," Suran said. "Seven billion frightened people awakening at the same time into a world where the infrastructure barely supported that many people before it was left to decay by the Voidborn? It would mean bloodshed on a scale unprecedented in the history of humanity."

"So how do we wake them, Daniel?" Stirling said. "Or would you prefer Andrew or maybe Suran?"

"Daniel is the name you have always known me by," Suran replied. "I see no need to change that now."

"Except it isn't your name, not really," Stirling replied. "I would have helped you, you know. If you'd told me the truth. I always wondered how you managed to be one step ahead of my thinking when we worked together. I understand now. I must have seemed like a child to you."

"Not at all," Suran replied. "Your intuitive understanding of Voidborn technology was impressive. You forget that I had slept for eons before I met you. I was not familiar with much of the technology they were sharing with their human allies in the Foundation. Without you we would never have perfected the implant technology that protects those children from Voidborn slavery."

"To think I operated on you to remove your implant," Stirling said, shaking his head. "You never even needed it, did you? Not to mention the fact that you could have just reached into your head and handed it to me, given your true nature."

"That would perhaps have rather startled you," Suran replied. "There were many things I was forced to do to keep my true identity a secret. The only person who knew the truth was Talon. If we had been discovered, we would have been forced back into hiding at best, hunted down and destroyed at worst. You know that. I didn't keep things from you because I didn't trust you; I didn't tell you because it was the only way to keep you safe. If the Foundation and the Voidborn had learned of our existence, there would have been nowhere safe to hide for anyone we had ever known or cared about. That may have mattered little to Talon, but for me it was not an option. I had allowed myself to become too fond of humanity and the new life they had afforded me."

"So, how *do* we save them?" Stirling asked. "How do you wake up seven billion people?"

"Slowly and carefully, my friend," Suran replied, "slowly and carefully."

Back in the rear compartment Sam handed the weapons to Rachel, Jay, and Mag.

"Don't take any unnecessary risks. For us to have any chance of this working, I need you all in one piece," Sam said, "and try to keep Stirling alive as well. I know he can be a bit of a pain in the backside sometimes, but he does have his uses."

"Message received loud and clear, boss," Jay said with a grin.

"I'm not your boss," Sam said.

"Yeah you are," Rachel said, smiling at him, "even if you don't want to admit it."

"I still think you're crazy," Mag said, shaking her head. "You do realize that there are about ten thousand things that could go wrong with this brilliant plan, don't you?"

"That's better than usual," Jay said, "much better, actually."

"We're approaching the Mothership," Stirling said as he walked into the compartment. "You three had better come with me."

"The Mothership has brought us into its landing pattern," Suran said. "It is time."

Jay, Rachel, and Mag followed Stirling into the forward

compartment. Suran turned toward Sam as he approached.

"Time to get this show on the road," Sam said.

"Before we do, I want you to know that I love you as much as I would have loved any biological child," Suran said, "and I am truly proud of the young man that you have become."

"I know," Sam replied, looking into the alien creature's eyes and finally seeing his father looking back at him. "Though, if I were you, it's not me I'd be worried about, it's Mom. She'll kill you when she finds out who you really are."

Suran let out a booming laugh. "Indeed," he said, smiling at Sam. "As you humans say, I believe that we should cross that particular bridge when we come to it."

Suran closed his eyes and dematerialized into a cloud of dust that spread out until it was barely visible, hanging in the air. A moment later Sam felt a soft thud through the soles of his boots as the drop-ship touched down, and the hatch in the side of the vessel hissed open, light streaming inside from the hangar beyond. Within seconds a pair of floating Voidborn Hunters entered the drop-ship, the green light that flickered across their silvery shells a sudden unpleasant reminder of his life in London after the invasion. Once these creatures had been a source of nightmares and now, as Sam stepped toward them confidently, he hoped that his voice wouldn't betray any of the fear that he felt in the pit of his stomach.

"My name is Sam Riley, I was responsible for the capture of your ship above London and I want to speak to the intelligence controlling this vessel."

Talon stood on the central control platform, feeling the flow of information from the vessel around him. It had taken time for him to adjust to the overwhelming stream of data, but he had adapted. The Grendels massed in the hangars far below him were simple hulking creatures that needed only the most uncomplicated of instructions. He would release them as a tide of blind destruction when the time came, allowing the rudimentary artificial intelligences that controlled them to make the simple decisions that would be all that his battle plan required. The smaller Voidborn Drones would keep the vessel functioning for as long as possible. The assault craft waiting in their hangars would provide air cover for the primary weapon at his disposal, the Mothership itself.

The escape of the prisoners had been a minor inconvenience. He was now within reach of victory and final retribution against his most hated enemy. As a commander of the Illuminate fleet he had seen the horrors that the Voidborn had wrought across the stars and he did not understand why they had spared the Earth from such wanton destruction. He told himself that, really, it did not matter. When he was finished, all would be ashes and the war would finally be over. The Voidborn would perish and the last remnant of his people would be safe forever.

He looked through the screens providing a view out over the superstructure of the Mothership, beyond which lay the inky blackness of space. Hanging there in the void, filling half his field of vision, was the bright blue surface of the Earth. He had risked drawing the Voidborn's attention by leaving the atmosphere, but it had dramatically reduced the journey time to his target. He issued a mental command to the Mothership's engines and the massive vessel began to drop out of orbit, gathering speed as it succumbed to the gentle but irresistible force of the Earth's gravity. A minute later the first flares of bright red plasma formed along the curved leading edge of the giant ship when it struck the first wispy layers of the atmosphere at phenomenal speed. The Mothership's systems reported that the angle of re-entry was too steep, that the energy shields would struggle to keep the vessel safe from the ferocious temperatures that were building outside. None of that mattered to Talon. All that did matter was that in a matter of minutes he would catch his enemy unaware and finally his vengeance would be complete.

Sam walked into the control room of the Voidborn Mothership, a Hunter on either side of him restraining his arms. Standing in the center of the room was a pedestal identical to the one he knew from the London Mothership. On it stood a matte black, featureless cylinder, nearly ten feet tall with glowing cables leading away from it and down into the bottomless pit. As the Hunters held him in place ten yards away, the surface of the cylinder began to ripple gently and then it suddenly exploded into a swirling cloud of black dust.

Sam had seen this transformation once before and he fought to keep his expression calm as the cloud quickly coalesced into a tall male figure. Other than the fact that its skin looked as if it were made from highly polished black obsidian, he suddenly realized it bore an uncanny resemblance to one of the Illuminate. The Voidborn looked down at Sam, its eyes glowing with green light, leaving twisting motes of black dust trailing behind it in the air as it moved toward him.

"You are known to us, human," it said. Its deep sonorous voice had a strange, vaguely digital sounding edge to it. "You are the one that severed our connection to the sixth. I will not allow you to do the same to the first. You will not corrupt this vessel. I will not allow the contamination of the Illuminate to spread any further. You will be cast into the singularity that powers this vessel, nothing less than total obliteration will suffice."

"I'm not part of the Illuminate," Sam said, "but they are coming and they mean to destroy you. That's what I came here to warn you about."

"The Illuminate are long dead," the Voidborn said, stepping closer to Sam. "You are the one remnant of their existence. We have purged the universe of their corruption. They are no longer any threat to us."

"You're wrong," Sam said, "and do you know how I know that? Because my dad told me."

The two Hunters holding Sam released their hold on his arms and their gleaming silver shells seemed to shimmer for a second before exploding into a seething cloud of silver dust, which coalesced into a humanoid shape. Suran materialized next to Sam. The flowing robes he had worn before were gone, replaced with gleaming white armor. The Voidborn's glowing eyes widened in surprise and it took a single step backward. Suran strode forward, reaching out and grabbing the creature's throat with his hand. The Voidborn let out a strangled digital screech, and small sections of its skin exploded in puffs of black smoke as it tried desperately to shift its shape, but the tiny streams of dust were sucked back into its body as Suran held his grip.

"Now, Sam," Suran yelled, "quickly, while it's form-locked."

Sam ran toward Suran and grabbed his outstretched hand. The process was instantaneous and overwhelming. Sam felt himself become one with the enormous vessel around him, feeling every pulse of energy through its colossal superstructure as if it were a signal racing through his own nervous system. He could feel every drop-ship soaring over the city below, every Hunter silently working to maintain the Mothership, every Grendel patrolling the streets. There was no way his human mind could cope with the sudden crushing wave of sensation that washed over him.

In the control room, Suran's fist closed on empty air as the Voidborn disintegrated, slipping between his fingers like grains of sand and falling to the floor in a pile of black and silver dust. He turned and caught Sam as his son's legs gave way beneath him, gently lowering him to the floor. Sam lay convulsing, his nervous system now just ablaze with a million different contradictory sensations.

"Come on, Sam," Suran said, looking at the agonized expression on his son's face and gently placing his hand on the side of the boy's head, "let me in."

Sam was drowning in a swirling tempest of sensory data. Suddenly, the volume of the mental static that surrounded him decreased and he sensed a presence nearby. A figure materialized from the swirl of colors and noise around him.

"Dad?" Sam said.

"No, child of Earth," the figure said. Sam couldn't make out who it was. He could make out just a blurred outline. "You will know me soon enough." The figure seemed to grow before him, darkening, its outline traced by crimson flames. "You will watch as I render your world unto ash. You and all of your kind will die screaming my name."

The figure reached out and Sam felt a moment of blind

animal panic as it seemed to grow impossibly large, swallowing him whole. Sam screamed in terror when he felt an instant of the pure, cold malevolence that surrounded him. The world rushed back in a flash of light. Sam blinked rapidly a few times and Suran's concerned face came into focus above him.

"Welcome back," Suran said. "I have control."

Sam slowly climbed to his feet with Suran's help and looked around the control room. The lights running through the walls now pulsed with a soft yellow glow. The Mothership was theirs.

"I saw something," Sam said, his voice shaky. "There's something else out there."

"More Voidborn?" Suran asked.

"No," Sam said, feeling a chill run down his spine at the memory, "not Voidborn, worse. Much worse."

"What do you mean?"

"I felt it for a moment," Sam said. "Whatever it is, it hates us more than you could possibly imagine."

"Are you sure you're okay?" Suran said. "The Illuminate interface to these vessels was not designed for human neural physiology. You may just have suffered sensory overload, which can induce extremely intense visions. I remember my first experience of the interface with the Illuminate—it was similarly powerful."

"I suppose," Sam said, rubbing his temples. "We need to get ready. Talon will be here soon."

"Indeed," Suran said. "You and your friends should prepare yourselves also. We may not have much—"

Suran stopped as the cables around the control panel snaked their way up his legs and under the plates of his armor.

"By the Illuminate," Suran said, his eyes suddenly wide with shock, "he's here."

# 11

Talon smiled as his Mothership sliced through the layer of cloud above the city, its leading edge still glowing bright orange from its near suicidal re-entry to the Earth's atmosphere. Damage reports streamed into his mind from the systems that had been compromised by the superheated plasma when the Mothership's energy shields had finally given way, but the vessel had survived and now the element of surprise was his. The Voidborn would never have expected a Mothership to attack from such an angle or at such speed and, as any true warrior knew, catching one's enemy unaware was to have already won half the battle.

He gave the mental command to launch the Mothership's entire fleet of drop-ships, streams of the sleek triangular aircraft pouring out of the hangars and screaming down toward their pre-assigned targets. Talon suddenly realized the power that the Voidborn had always had. The underlying technology may originally have been Illuminate, but the modifications the Voidborn had made in order to turn them into weapons to be used against their own creators were formidable. Their forces were powerful, vast, and unquestioningly obedient, without any trace of fear. This power was magnificent.

As the first drop-ships began their attack runs, Talon saw the rippling waves of blue energy that spread out across its energy shields when the massive vessel tried to absorb or redirect as much of the destructive force as it could. There were no enemy aircraft rising from the hangars of the Voidborn Mothership and he could not help feel a slight sense of surprise. He may have had the drop on them, but if there was one thing that he'd learned from his many previous battles with the Voidborn, it was that they were never slow to react. He ignored the moment of doubt and mentally issued the command for the ground forces awaiting deployment to prepare to drop. Satisfied that everything was ready, his gaze turned back to the Mothership hanging in the center of the view screens in front of him.

"All batteries," he said with a smile, "open fire."

Sam felt the first shudders of impact through the soles of his feet as he ran down the spiraling concourse that surrounded the Mothership's central power core. He could hear the rumble of distant explosions and he noticed the huge crystal column that ran up to the power distribution hub flaring with unusually bright light as the giant ship's core struggled to provide the energy shields with the power they required. Talon had arrived hours earlier than they had expected and Sam suddenly felt a twinge of doubt as it sank in that they were going up against one of the Illuminate's greatest military commanders, someone who had spent most of his life fighting the Voidborn. He found himself wondering if their plan really had any chance.

There was a burst of much louder explosions from above. He kept running, finally sprinting into the hangar where the drop-ship that had smuggled them on board was sitting in the center of the landing pad. The surrounding drop-ships slowly lifted from the ground and headed for the glowing force field that separated the hangar from the open air beyond, ready for combat. Sam glanced over at the cloudless sky on the other side of the force field and saw several enemy drop-ships streak past outside, their hulls glowing with the blue lights that indicated they were part of Talon's forces.

Sam ran to the stationary drop-ship and into the empty passenger compartment. "I'm inside," Sam said to the air. "Let them out."

Suddenly the bulkhead at the far end of the drop-ship melted away to reveal Stirling, Rachel, Jay, and Mag.

The false wall that Suran had willed into existence before they'd landed faded away in a glittering shimmer as the structural nanites were absorbed back into the bulkhead.

"If I wasn't claustrophobic before, I am now," Jay said. "What the hell's going on out there?"

"Talon's here," Sam said. "We have to move."

"Already?" Stirling said, sounding shocked, as the five of them headed to the hangar deck.

"Two minutes earlier and the Voidborn would still have been in control of this ship," Sam said as he looked up at the four huge metallic pods that were being lowered into place at the far end of the hangar. "At the moment, if I'm honest, I'm not sure if that's a good thing or a bad thing."

Suddenly the biggest explosion yet came from somewhere high above them and they all staggered, trying to keep their balance as the deck lurched beneath their feet. They had to take the fight to Talon now.

"Doctor Stirling, I think Suran's going to need your help with damage control," Sam said as something detonated with a bang on the surface of the vessel far above them, sending a stream of sparks cascading to the floor below.

"I'll head to the control room," Stirling said. "I'm not sure how much I can help him. Let's hope I won't have to. Be careful, all of you."

He looked at the four of them for a moment and then gave a quick nod, and hurried out of the hangar.

"Okay, let's do this," Sam said, turning to the four giant containers. A moment later, the pods slowly hissed open simultaneously. The smoke inside cleared to reveal four dormant Grendels. "Ready when you are."

The first Grendel flared into life and stepped toward Sam. He swallowed nervously as it looked down at him. A moment later the Grendel's chest opened like a clam shell to reveal a large cavity. Black tentacles slithered out and wrapped themselves around Sam's waist lifting him into the air and placing him gently inside the cavity. Sam watched as the other Grendels followed suit, lifting his friends up gently and placing them inside their armored shells.

A moment later the Grendel's chest cavity hissed closed again and Sam found himself in perfect darkness, the only sound his own breathing. He felt a warm sensation creeping up his legs then up past his waist and over his chest. Suran had warned him what to expect, but it didn't make it feel any less weird. Then he felt the warm, sticky gel that he was suspended within ooze over his face, filling his nose and mouth. He fought to control a rising tide of panic as the liquid filled his throat and then his lungs. Every instinct screamed at him to get out as he felt a horrid momentary drowning sensation and then his senses flared back into life. He was standing in the hangar bay, his viewpoint unusually elevated. He lifted his hand and looked at the massive razor-clawed fist in front of his face. A grin spreading across his face, he took a step forward and felt the thudding impact of his own footsteps as the Grendel that was now just an extension of his own body stepped out of the storage pod. They'd known that the Voidborn had twisted the Illuminate colony ships to suit their own sinister purposes, but it was not until Suran had explained the Grendels' true purpose that what Suran had planned made sense. The Grendels had not been created as the monstrous warriors they had become—they had been designed to allow the Illuminate manning the colony vessels to explore planets with extreme hostile environments. They were never intended to be soldiers—they were meant to be suits of armor.

"This . . . is . . . wicked," Jay said in Sam's ear as the Mothership hooked up their communications net.

"And to think that I spent all that time trying *not* to end up inside one of these things," Rachel said.

Sam turned and watched as the other three Grendels stepped out of their pods and looked around the hangar. Sam couldn't believe how intuitive his control of the Grendel felt; it really was simply an extension of his own body.

"Thought I'd already had my quota of weird for the week," Mag said, flexing the massive claws of her Grendel. "Looks like I was wrong."

"Okay, Mothership, we are ready for launch," Sam said.

"Understood," Suran replied, "maneuvering us into position now."

Up in the control room Suran gave the Mothership a series of commands. He felt the enormous vessel's anti-gravity engines fire, pushing it slowly toward Talon's ship, the energy shields flaring as the other Mothership's barrage of fire intensified. They only had seconds until the primary shields gave way.

Down on the hangar deck Sam's Grendel stomped toward the force field at the other end of the bay as more drop-ships shot past overhead, zooming outside to join the battle. He approached the edge and peered out at the breathtaking scene beyond. The air was filled with drop-ships locked in life-or-death dogfights, streams of cannon fire reaching out and filling the sky with black clouds of spinning debris. They maneuvered as only digital pilots could, pulling off impossible turns and rolls as they fought to bring their weapons to bear on one another. To Sam they looked like massive flocks of birds swooping through the air in ever-changing clouds, lit from within by the flares of explosions and weapons fire.

Talon's Mothership was now less than two hundred yards away and only fifty yards below as Suran pushed their Mothership upward, climbing to get above it. The torrent of blue energy bolts that streamed from the gun emplacements all over the upper surface of the Mothership intensified, splashing against their own ship's energy shields, which flickered just for a moment and then suddenly gave way. The hail of enemy fire tore into the superstructure of their ship and the series of explosions that followed sent massive blazing chunks of the superstructure tumbling toward the city below.

"Go, now!" Suran said in his ear. Sam looked down at the fifty-yard drop to Talon's Mothership below and took a deep breath. Then he jumped. The Grendel dropped like a stone, in freefall for just a couple of seconds before slamming into the Mothership, the black hull cratering beneath its massive clawed feet. Sam took two strides toward the energy cannon next to which he had landed and ripped it from its mounting with a grunt, flinging it with as much force as he could at a nearby gun emplacement, smiling as it hit home with a crunch. Beside him the other three Grendels landed with a shuddering impact that would have killed any of their pilots inside if it were not for the impact-absorbing gel in which they were all immersed. Sam looked up at the central spire that dominated the superstructure of Talon's vessel. That was their target, about a mile and a half away.

"Let's move!" Sam yelled, glancing up at their Mothership. Secondary explosions flared all over the heavily damaged sections. Time was running out.

Talon smiled as he saw the Voidborn Mothership's shields finally give way. He had expected a more concerted counterattack. He supposed that the last thing they had expected was anyone on this backward planet who would be capable of fighting back. Today they would learn the error of their ways.

"Stop this, Talon." The incoming transmission came from the Voidborn Mothership. A moment later a blue semi-transparent hologram of Suran appeared, hovering in the air in front of him. "Please, we already have enough blood on our hands."

"Why have you done this?" Talon asked, realizing immediately what had happened. "By taking control of that ship, you've doomed yourself. I have no choice but to destroy you."

"Of course you do," Suran replied. "This is madness. Destroying the Voidborn and slaughtering another species in the process won't bring our people back. You must see that."

"Our people are long dead, Suran—you know that as well as I do," Talon said. "All that remains is duty. Duty to the memory of the Illuminate and to seeing that justice is done. The Voidborn die this day."

"You know I will die before I let you murder billions of innocents again," Suran said, shaking his head.

"I know, old friend," Talon replied. "I will mourn you. Good-bye."

With a quick mental command, he severed the link.

"Launch all ground forces," Talon said. "Attack the central control node—this ends now."

"So how the hell do we get up there?" Jay asked, looking at the crystalline spire towering above them.

"We climb," Sam said, slamming the claws of his Grendel's right hand into the surface of the spire and dragging himself upward. "Come on."

Around them the swarming dogfight between the two Motherships' air forces lit up the sky with energy bolts and the sudden bright flares of drop-ships exploding into clouds of tumbling, burning debris. Talon's Mothership continued its barrage of fire on Suran's vessel. The return fire seemed weaker now, and the shields on Talon's ship continued to absorb it, meaning it was sustaining minimal damage. The battle seemed to be tipping decisively in his favor.

Sam tried to climb faster, but the Grendel was not built for speed. Sam winced as the surface of the spire exploded in a shower of glinting fragments just a few yards above his head. An enemy drop-ship rocketed past, its other shots going just wide as it banked around for another pass. Sam let go with the Grendel's left claw and swung across the spire, losing his grip for an instant before his claws again found purchase, leaving long scratches in the surface of the structure as he slid downward a couple of yards. A split second later the spot where he'd been hanging just a moment before was reduced to a glowing molten crater as another barrage of fire from the drop-ship slammed into it. The ship came around again, more slowly this time, floating toward the four climbing Grendels, bringing its weapons to bear as it drew to within ten yards of them. They were sitting ducks.

"Screw this," Jay said under his breath, and he leaped from the tower, slamming into the drop-ship, his Grendel's claws fighting to hold on to the smooth armored skin of the aircraft. The drop-ship lurched crazily as Jay slashed at its hull, digging through the armor in an attempt to reach some of the more vulnerable components that lay beneath.

"Jay, get out of there!" Sam yelled, watching as the ship began to spiral out of control, dropping away from them.

Jay felt the vessel tip beneath him and he clung desperately as it rolled over on to one side, spiraling downward at terrifying speed. The superstructure of the Mothership vanished from beneath them as the fatally damaged drop-ship shot out over the city far below on a wildly erratic and uncontrolled trajectory. It suddenly flipped one hundred and eighty degrees and the single claw by which Jay's Grendel hung on lost its purchase. He reached desperately for anything to grab on to, but gravity had him now and there was a sickening lurch in his stomach as he tumbled in freefall toward the city below.

"Damn it," Jay said in Sam's ear, his voice strained. "Go get him, guys. See you on the other—"

There was a sudden burst of static and then silence.

"JAY!" Sam yelled, but there was no response. His friend was gone.

"Oh God, no," Rachel whispered in Sam's ear.

Sam felt a moment of overwhelming grief, but still he knew what had to be done. He swallowed the gut-wrenching loss mixed with rage and stared at the top of the spire fifty yards above him. Talon was waiting for him up there and Sam was going to make him pay for everything he'd done.

Talon watched with satisfaction as the first drop-ships carrying his ground forces began to leave their hangars. Once Suran's Mothership was defeated, there would be nothing to stop his assault on the primary control node. When that fell, it would mean the end of the Voidborn forever. He understood the cost to the humans and their planet, and it was still a price he was happy to pay.

He closed his eyes, allowing the three-dimensional map of the city to form in his mind's eye, and plotted the routes of his forces' advance.

A sudden noise caught his attention and he opened his eyes just in time to see the massive shape of Sam's Grendel loom in front of the floor-to-ceiling windows on the other side of the control room. The Grendel drew back its massive fist and smashed it into the reinforced glass, sending a spider web of cracks dancing across its surface. The massive figure punched the window again and it exploded inward, thick chunks of glass scattering over the control-room floor.

The Grendel ripped aside the tattered remains of the window, ducking under the frame and stepping into the room. Talon gave a mental command and the cables that connected him to the control pedestal disconnected and slid away, slithering back under the platform. He took a single step toward the Grendel as two more of the monstrous machines climbed into the room behind it.

"It's over, Talon," Sam said, his voice amplified by the Grendel's systems.

"Do you truly believe that?" Talon said with a smile. "I have fought the Voidborn on a hundred worlds. I have seen them lay waste to entire star systems. Do you really think you can threaten me, boy?"

Talon's shape began to shift. He grew three feet in height, his armor thickening, the plates sliding over each other and interlocking as a smooth, white, featureless mask closed over his face. His right forearm grew longer and longer, stretching into a six-foot-long blade that crackled with blue energy.

"Suran was a fool to send you here," Talon said, taking another step toward Sam's Grendel. "Nothing can stop me now, certainly not you."

"We'll see," Sam said, swiping at him with the Grendel's massive claws.

Talon ducked, bringing his blade up in a sweeping arc

that sliced the Grendel's hand off cleanly at the wrist. Sam staggered backward, instinctively grabbing at the severed stump that was now squirting green-black liquid. He knew logically that it wasn't his hand, but his neural connection to the Grendel made it feel all too real, despite the lack of pain.

Mag came at Talon from the side, moving faster than Sam and dealing Talon a vicious backhand blow, which struck him in the shoulder and sent him flying across the room. He slid to a halt and leaped to his feet in one fluid motion, raising the blade in front of him defensively as Mag came after him, her Grendel's stomping feet leaving shattered footprints in the deck. Talon ran toward her, sliding under the stampeding bio-mechanical machine as its claws slashed through the empty air where he had been standing just a split second before. He brought his blade around in a glowing arc, slicing through the exposed muscular cable on the back of the Grendel's leg. Mag's Grendel dropped to one knee, instantly crippled, her momentum carrying her forward and sending her slamming face first into the ground.

Talon stepped toward Mag's fallen Grendel and lifted the blade high above his head, ready to deliver a killing blow. Sam raised his one good claw and willed the suit's systems to respond. A black tentacle shot across the room and wrapped around Talon's wrist, tightening as Sam yanked his arm back hard. Talon staggered backward, turning toward Sam as a shorter glowing blue blade materialized on the back of his free wrist. He brought the blade swinging upward and sliced through the tentacle with one slash, the severed end slipping from his sword arm and falling twitching to the floor.

Talon gave a simple mental command and two black-shelled Hunters rose from the pit on either side of the control pedestal. They fired bright blue bolts of light, slamming into Sam's shoulder armor and blowing it to pieces. He staggered backward and Rachel stomped forward, grabbing the closest of the two Hunters, her massive hand crushing the Hunter with a sickening cracking squelch, its black and silver blood oozing between the Grendel's claws. The other Hunter fired again, the bolt sizzling through the air and striking Sam's Grendel in the chest. Inside Sam felt real pain, a burning sensation in the side of his chest where the bolt had penetrated his armor.

Rachel flung the remains of the crushed Hunter in her Grendel's claw at the other Drone, sending it spinning into the wall with a crunch and sliding to the floor, its tentacles twitching. Sam gritted his teeth as Talon walked calmly toward him, dragging the tip of his blade along the floor, leaving a trail of blue sparks in his wake.

"This was Suran's plan?" Talon said, his voice dripping with contempt. "To send children to stop me? I wonder if he knew he was sending you to your deaths."

Rachel stepped in front of Sam, raising her Grendel's claws in front of her.

"You think you can defeat me?" Talon said as Rachel's Grendel took a step toward him.

"No," Rachel replied, "but I can distract you."

Talon spun around, a split second too slow to react. The fist of Mag's Grendel hit him square in the chest and he flew across the room, slamming into the wall with a crunch. Mag tried to go after him, but her movement was painfully slow, her Grendel dragging its crippled leg behind it as she moved. Rachel stomped toward Talon as he dragged himself into a sitting position, coughing and spitting out a mouthful of pale blue blood. She stood over the fallen alien, one of the last of his kind, and looked down at him as he raised one hand, as if asking her to wait before delivering the killing blow.

"This is for Jay," Rachel said, raising her clawed fist. Talon vanished in the blink of an eye, replaced by a swirling cloud of dust that rushed between the legs of Rachel's Grendel and coalesced back into the form of the Illuminate warrior, weapon raised. Talon drove his sword through the back of Rachel's Grendel and it emerged from the giant armored creature's chest, dripping red. Rachel gasped once, looking down at the protruding blade, and then with a final strangled gurgle her Grendel fell forward, slamming to the ground and lying still.

Sam ran at Talon as he pulled his sword from the fallen

Grendel, screaming in rage, ignoring the searing pain in his side. Talon sidestepped the charging Grendel like a bull fighter, bringing his blade around in a sweeping arc that severed the machine's leg at the hip. Sam tumbled forward and slid into Rachel's immobile Grendel, slimy black liquid spraying from the severed stump of its leg.

Mag limped toward the Illuminate warrior as he turned to face the advancing bio-machine.

"Take one more step and he dies," Talon said, placing the tip of his sword in the middle of Sam's Grendel's back.

Mag froze. She knew that Talon was not bluffing.

"Kneel," Talon said.

Mag's crippled Grendel dropped to its knees as Talon walked toward her. He said nothing, just swept his sword around in an arc that sliced the Grendel's bestial head clean off its shoulders. The Grendel's chest immediately popped open and Mag slid out, falling to the ground, retching and coughing, covered in the slimy residue of the protective gel that she had been floating in just seconds before.

"The hybrid," Talon said, "not quite one thing or the other. It will be a kindness putting you out of your misery."

Mag staggered to her feet, Talon towering over her. She looked up at the featureless white glass of his helmet and snarled. Behind Talon the chest of Sam's Grendel hissed open.

"Someone once told me that I'd know a monster

when I saw one," Mag said, "and she was right."

Talon's helmet slid back as he looked down at Mag with a vicious smile.

"After today there will be no more monsters," he said, raising his sword.

Sam pressed his hand against the side of Talon's head.

"Now," Sam whispered.

Mag sprang upward, her claws swiping through the air, slashing at Talon's neck. Talon staggered backward, his hand flying to the vicious wound. He looked confused for a moment and then, for the first time, Sam saw fear in his eyes.

"What did you do to me?" Talon gasped, staggering backward.

"My father called it form-lock," Sam said. "How does it feel to be mortal?"

"You filthy little ape," Talon spat, the blood now running down over the chest plate of his armor. "Do you really think this will make any difference? Do you think you've won?"

"I don't really care," Sam said, "as long as I get to watch you die."

Mag let out a low growl and swiped again at Talon. He turned and ran toward the shattered windows on the other side of the room before leaping into the void. A moment later a drop-ship rose up above the window with Talon clinging to its upper surface. Mag sprinted toward the window, but the ship banked away too quickly, leaving a gap between her and her fleeing prey that was too wide for even her to jump. She watched helplessly as the aircraft flew away, heading for the city below.

"Help me!" Sam yelled, trying desperately to pull the chest of Rachel's Grendel open. Mag ran over and joined him, using her enhanced strength to wrench the black armored plates apart. Rachel's still body slid out of the cavity within. There was a horrible-looking wound in her abdomen and Sam could already see that there was far too much blood mixed in with the protective gel. Rachel coughed once, the gel dribbling out of the corner of her mouth as her eyes flickered open.

"Did we stop him?" Rachel asked, her voice small and weak.

"Yes," Sam said, "we stopped him."

"You always were a crappy liar, Riley," Rachel said, her voice growing fainter.

"We'll get you out of here—you're going to be okay," Mag said.

"And you're not much better," Rachel said, looking at Mag with a pained smile that turned into a wince. She looked back at Sam. "You stop him, Sam. For me, for Jay, you . . . stop . . ."

Her eyes suddenly looked as if she were focusing on something far beyond Sam, and then the light went out of them. Sam hugged his friend's body to his chest, feeling hot tears running down his cheeks. He did not know how much more pain he could endure.

"We have to go after him," Mag said, putting her hand on Sam's shoulder.

"I know," Sam replied. "Nobody kills him but me."

Suddenly, they both felt the Mothership lurch beneath their feet as it changed course and began to accelerate. Sam looked out through the shattered windows and saw the Tokyo Mothership glide into view. There were huge black gashes in its upper surface from which billowing clouds of glowing smoke were pouring. The barrage of fire from Talon's Mothership had ceased and now it was accelerating toward the other giant vessel, the distance between them closing at an ever-increasing rate.

"He's going to ram the other Mothership," Sam said. "We have to warn my dad."

"How?" Mag asked.

"I don't know," Sam said, looking frantically around the room. He gently laid Rachel's body down on the floor and walked over to his own fallen Grendel. The damage to the bio-mechanical machine was catastrophic, but he knew it should still have some residual power reserves. He reached down and placed his hand on the Grendel's smooth black armored skin and mentally activated his implant. He felt himself connecting to the Mothership's command and control net, and then with a small mental nudge he reached out for his father.

*He's going to ram your Mothership,* Sam said, the message forming in his mind.

*Yes, I feared that was his intention,* Suran replied.

*I have no way of stopping him,* Sam said. *He escaped— he's heading for the city.*

*His control of the Mothership will weaken at increased range,* Suran said. *That may offer us an opportunity. You have to try to wrest control of the vessel from him.*

*How?* Sam asked. *I've always needed something or someone else to act as an interface. I can't do it alone.*

*I'm sorry, Sam,* Suran replied in his head. *I don't know. You must act quickly; my vessel has sustained too much damage. It was as I feared—I was no match for Talon in battle. I cannot hope to outrun you.*

Sam glanced out of the window. The other Mothership was already noticeably closer as they both drifted out over the waters of Tokyo Bay. He ran to the control pedestal and reached down, touching the floor and probing mentally with his implant for any weakness within the control systems. It was no good: the vessel was silent to him. His father may have been right about Talon's control diminishing, but there was still a solid wall between Sam and the vessel.

He turned around and surveyed the scene of devastation in the control room, looking at the three fallen

Grendels and Mag kneeling down next to the body of one of his closest friends, brushing a stray strand of hair off her pale forehead. He looked past them at the Mothership looming ever closer through the windows beyond and he felt a moment of despair. Then, seeing his own footprints in the dirty yellow dust that covered the floor in front of the control pedestal, his heart suddenly leaped. He touched the fine powder, feeling a tiny flicker of something at the edge of his mind. He closed his eyes and reached out for the barely noticeable trace of energy that still lingered.

Mag watched Sam drop to his knees and place both hands on the ground in front of him, his eyes closed. A second or two later the yellow dust began to rise into the air, swirling around him in an ever-thickening cloud. She felt a shudder of impact run through the massive vessel's superstructure as the leading edge of Talon's Mothership grated over the upper surface of Suran's ship, their hulls shredding each other as they ground together in a hideous slow-motion collision.

An instant later the cloud of dust surrounding Sam flared with a bright yellow light and a figure began to form. Mag struggled to stand, the floor beneath bucking as the two Motherships drove into each other, flaming debris tumbling away beneath them and slamming into the streets below like high-explosive bombs.

The golden figure finally coalesced in front of Sam,

her eyes glowing with yellow light, and he reached out and placed his hand on the side of her head.

"I have control," the Servant said calmly. The massive anti-gravity engines that powered the Mothership changed the direction of their impulses and slowly but surely the two Motherships began to separate with the terrible screeching sound of disintegrating superstructure. A minute later, they both hung over the bay, smoke pouring from the tangled wreckage that had been left behind by their collision . . . but still airborne.

"It's good to see you again," Sam said. "Where is Talon?"

"I am working to subvert his control of the Mothership's ancillary units," the Servant said. "He has full command of this vessel's land and air units."

"Can you break his control?" Sam said.

"No," the Servant replied, "Talon must relinquish his hold on the Mothership's systems."

"Or die," Mag said, walking toward them.

"Indeed," the Servant replied, "his termination would also achieve the same result."

"Good," Sam said, his expression grim. "Can you connect me to the Illuminate called Suran who is in control of the other Mothership?"

"Yes, one moment," the Servant replied. "Connection established."

"Well done, Sam," Suran said, his voice coming from

the air around them. "A few more seconds and I do not believe we would have been able to remain in the air. I assume you have control of Talon's vessel?"

"Only partial control," Sam replied. "He's still in command of the drop-ships and his ground forces."

"What can I do to help?" Suran asked.

"We need you to send a drop-ship," Sam said. "Now."

# 12

Talon stepped on to the street. The battle was raging at the far end. Grendels lit in blue and yellow tore into each other, slamming into shopfronts and office buildings, fighting with the savagery of wild beasts. Above them Hunters were swooping between the lamp posts and electrical cables, their energy cannons blazing. The trail of destruction that led to the ongoing battle was clear evidence of the progress that Talon's forces had made against Suran's defenders. He could still feel his connection to the network that was allowing him to control his troops, and the longer he spent in command of them the more they began to feel like an extension of his own will. Suran was no warrior and Talon had fought more battles than he cared to remember. It would not be long until the Voidborn control node fell to them.

He reached into one of the pouches that hung around

the waist of his armor and pulled out a small transparent bag filled with blue gel. Tearing open the bag, he daubed the gel over the vicious neck wound that the Vore hybrid had given him. The gel hardened almost instantly, sealing the wound, but he had already lost a considerable amount of blood. The only way to heal himself properly was to reverse the form-lock under which the boy had placed him—until then he was trapped in his current form, and vulnerable. The reversal could only happen if another member of the Illuminate was to remove the lock, not something that either the boy or Suran would ever willingly do.

He winced as the chemicals within the gel accelerated his healing process. It had been a long time since anything or anyone had actually hurt him. It hardly mattered now, he thought to himself as he looked up at the giant tower looming over them. Soon his forces would have control of the primary node and his mortality would be irrelevant. He flinched slightly as a drop-ship shot past overhead, its energy cannons laying down a devastating field of fire that scattered the last few units defending the entrance to the Skytree.

Talon reached into another pouch at his waist and pulled out a small disc, only four inches in diameter, that glowed with a soft blue light. He smiled to himself. This seemingly innocuous object was the key to his final victory. An instant later there was the sound of a drop-ship from somewhere behind him and Talon ducked involuntarily as it screamed past just a few yards overhead, its hull dancing with yellow light. The drop-ship opened fire on the other aircraft, its energy cannons flaring and sending crackling bolts tearing through its black, crystalline hull.

Talon's aircraft spun out of control, slamming into the ground and sliding into the advancing Grendels, knocking them flying before it pin-wheeled into an office building. It exploded with a bright blue flare of energy, scattering the tower's attackers and forcing Talon to duck for cover. With a low rumble, the twenty-story building collapsed in on itself, sending chunks of concrete scattering across the road and filling the air with billowing clouds of dust.

After a few seconds Talon climbed back to his feet and strained to see through the gray cloud that now filled the street ahead of him. He brought the forces around him closer, a pair of Grendels flanking him as he picked his way through the rubble that lay across the road, heading for the entrance to the tower. As the dust slowly cleared, he saw the drop-ship that had just attacked his forces sitting on the road in front of the entrance to the Skytree. Standing beside it were Suran, the boy, and the Vore hybrid.

"You're not going any farther," Sam said when Talon walked toward them, his glowing sword in his hand.

"You are proving harder to kill than I had imagined,"

Talon said as Grendels took up positions on either side of him. He reached for the Mothership with his mind and immediately realized that for whatever reason he could no longer access the vessel's control systems. "What have you done? Why can I no longer access the Voidborn vessel?"

"It is not too late. Lay down your weapons and accept the consequences of your actions," Suran said, stepping toward Talon.

"You always were an idealistic fool," Talon replied, sneering at Suran. He looked up at the Grendel standing to his left. "Kill them all."

The Grendel took a step toward them and roared. Suran stretched out his arm and it extended, slowly forming into a sword identical to the one Talon was holding.

"You are no warrior, Suran," Talon said. "You cannot win."

"Maybe," Suran replied, "but I shall die fighting."

The Grendel charged at Suran, and he ducked its wildly swinging claws, slashing at the creature's shoulder, his blade leaving a long glowing scar in its armor. The Grendel turned, its jaws snapping at empty air as Suran dodged beneath its attack, ducking under its arm and driving his sword into the creature's elbow joint. Black blood gushed onto the dusty road below. Suran spun around, his sword arcing toward the Grendel's back. At the precise instant his sword buried itself into the Grendel's spine, the monstrous creature's tail flashed through the air, its daggerlike tip burying itself in Suran's chest. It hoisted him off the ground before flinging him away across the street like a rag doll.

Sam ran over to his fallen father as the Grendel dropped to its knees, all control of its legs now lost. It tried to drag itself across the road for a few yards before it finally collapsed to the ground and lay still.

Sam crouched down next to Suran. His father looked up at him with a pained expression. Tiny wisps of dust writhed around the gaping hole in the front of his armor, proof of his body's doomed attempts to repair itself, despite the Voidborn nanites that were now swarming within the wound.

"He cannot be allowed to destroy the tower," Suran said, his voice strained.

"How do I stop him?" Sam asked, glancing over at Talon, who was watching them with a vicious smile on his face.

"You can't," Suran said, "but we can. Good-bye, my son. I love you."

Suran reached up and placed his hand gently on the side of Sam's head. Sam felt a moment of searing pain and was suddenly blinded by a flash of white light. He staggered backward, and Suran's body began to disintegrate into a pile of white dust. Sam's hands went to his head as he felt pressure building inside his skull. He dropped to his knees, feeling as if his head would burst. Slowly the pain subsided as he knelt panting in the street, his vision gradually returning to normal. He looked up just in time to see Mag charging at Talon, her fangs bared and claws outstretched.

"Mag, no!" Sam yelled.

Talon closed his eyes for an instant and the Grendel standing next to him stepped forward, a black tentacle shooting from its wrist and wrapping around one of Mag's ankles, sending her tumbling to the floor. The tentacle retracted, dragging Mag toward the Grendel as she thrashed wildly, slashing at the slimy tendril with her claws. The Grendel took three quick steps toward her and scooped her up off the ground, its massive claws closing around her neck as she struggled uselessly against its overwhelming strength. She dangled from the Grendel's outstretched hand, pulling at the black claws that tightened around her neck.

"Let her go!" Sam screamed, fighting the rising tide of despair he felt in his chest.

"On one condition," Talon said calmly. "Reverse the form-lock. Free me from the confines of this shape and I will spare her. Otherwise . . ."

Mag gave a strangled gasp of pain when the Grendel's claws tightened by just a tiny amount.

Sam looked at Mag and saw the mix of defiance and fear in her eyes. He had no choice. He walked toward Talon and placed his hand on the side of his head. A broad smile spread across Talon's face as he felt the restraints on his shape-shifting abilities fall away. The scratches and dents in his armor disappeared and the long claw-shaped gashes in his neck faded away, the hardened layer of medical gel falling to the ground.

"Thank you," Talon said. "That's so much better."

Sam looked at the fallen defenders of the tower that lay scattered on the street around them and then up at the dozens of Talon's drop-ships circling above before letting his head drop, knowing in that moment that they had lost. Nothing could stop Talon now.

"I was going to grant you a swift death," Talon said, "but now I think I might actually let you live. So much worse to be one of the final witnesses to the death of your world."

"Just get on with it," Sam said, his voice filled with resignation. "Destroy the tower."

"Oh, I'm not going to destroy it," Talon said with a smile. "If I'd wanted to do that, I would simply have flown the Mothership into it. No, I have something quite different in mind."

He grabbed Sam by the scruff of his neck and dragged him toward the entrance to the tower. The Grendel carrying Mag followed. A massive black sphere was nestled at the base of the tower within a spider's web of cables, all throbbing with red light. At the bottom of the sphere was a glowing red portal, its crimson light spilling out across the square. Talon dragged Sam toward the sphere and threw him to the ground just a couple of yards from the glowing hole in its base.

"Do you know what this is?" Talon asked, pointing at the bright opening. Sam shook his head as he slowly climbed to his feet. "This is a pattern interface," Talon continued. "The Voidborn use it to assimilate new technology, copying it and duplicating it across the entire fleet. During our war, they used them to copy any new weapons we used against them, before turning the very same weapons against us. It was part of the reason we could never defeat them, no matter what new technologies we devised. Suran saw a different use for it, though, a means by which we could wake the sleeping people of Earth and have them rise up against the Voidborn.

"His plan was simple: we would upload a modified design for their Drones, Hunters as you call them, that would unwittingly distribute Illuminate nanites to the sleeping humans in their charge, nanites that would wake them without actually severing their connection to the control network, leaving them unharmed, but still restoring their free will. The plan was elegant, the execution more problematic. When we first introduced the nanites to the enslaved humans we inadvertently created the Vore."

"My father was horrified by what you had done," Sam said. "It wasn't him that released those things in Edinburgh—it was you."

"Indeed it was," Talon said. "Your father wanted to go

back to the drawing board, try and find a way to wake the humans without turning them into monsters. He always was a naive fool. I saw the unmodified nanites' potential immediately. We could turn the humans against the Voidborn *now*. It was the only way to protect the Heart, to make sure that the Voidborn would never be able to erase the last remnant of the Illuminate. To me, the choice was clear. I form-locked Suran, placed him in confinement and then released the Vore in Edinburgh. They were more effective than I could ever have dreamed. All I needed then was a way to spread the Vore to every corner of the planet. Thankfully, your father had already created that."

Talon reached into the pouch at his waist and pulled out a glowing blue disc. "The nanites in this suspension field will implant a design for the Vore in the Voidborn creation matrix along with instructions for their Drones to distribute it among the entire population of enslaved humans. Every sleeping human on Earth will be transformed in a matter of days. The Voidborn will be destroyed by their own slaves. A rather fitting end, I think."

"You're insane," Sam said, "but that's no excuse for the thing you've become. You're worse than the Voidborn."

"You wouldn't say that if you had seen the things I have seen," Talon said, something cold and empty in his voice. "Enough talk. It is time." He walked toward the pattern interface, the blue disc sitting in the palm of his outstretched hand.

The wall of the glass walkway that ran alongside the plaza exploded as a Grendel smashed through it, landing with a crunch next to Talon and swatting him aside like a fly. Talon slammed into the wall on the other side of the plaza, momentarily stunned. The Grendel, lit with yellow light, turned toward Sam.

"Miss me?" Jay said before striding across the plaza toward the other towering creature that was still holding Mag. Talon's Grendel tossed the girl aside and Mag landed hard on the concrete twenty yards away. Jay's Grendel slammed into it, delivering a massive blow to the other creature's chest and sending it staggering backward. Jay pressed home his advantage, slashing at the other Grendel's face, his claws raking across its eyes. The other Grendel roared with rage, blinded and flailing as Jay side-stepped its wild uncontrolled swings.

Sam caught a movement out of the corner of his eye and saw Talon climbing to his feet before transforming in the blink of an eye into a swirling cloud of dust that raced toward Jay.

"Jay! Look out!" Sam yelled as he saw Talon materialize behind Jay, sword raised.

Something snapped inside Sam and he suddenly felt as if he were falling forward, but then he realized with a sudden jolt of disorientation that he wasn't falling—he was *flying* across the plaza toward Talon. He rematerialized between Talon and Jay's Grendel and the startled

Illuminate warrior backed away from him.

"That's not possible," Talon hissed, shock in his eyes. "You are not Illuminate."

"No, but my father was," Sam said, finally understanding what Suran had given him at the moment of his death. He shifted again into a swirling cloud of glowing yellow dust as the nanites that now composed his body raced toward Talon.

Talon too became incorporeal and the two of them merged together into a single swirling cloud. Jay slammed the blinded Grendel into the floor, reaching down and ripping the creature's head off with a sickening crunch. The decapitated creature thrashed for a moment and then lay still, green-black blood pooling on the floor beneath it.

Jay's Grendel walked toward Mag as she opened her eyes with a groan. She saw the advancing Grendel and scrambled backward, trying to get away from the monstrous creature.

"It's okay," Jay said. "It's me."

There was a fleeting look of confusion on Mag's face and then she let out a relieved sigh. She looked past the Grendel and at the swirling cloud, lit up by blue and yellow light, that hovered in the center of the square.

"What the hell is that?" Mag asked, her eyes wide.

"I have absolutely no idea," Jay said. He had only caught a glimpse of Talon and Sam before they had transformed into their current state. He watched helplessly, having no idea how he could possibly help his friend.

Sam felt a wild sense of disorientation as he fought with Talon. It was not a physical fight as much as a mental one, each probing the other for a gap in their defenses, their nanites attempting to assimilate each other and absorb one body within the other. He had no experience of this new form and Talon's centuries of practice were paying off. He could feel himself weakening, losing himself within the swirling mass. He gave a mental wrench and felt himself become solid again, falling out of the air and landing on the ground, flat on his back, all the wind knocked out of him. He rolled over, gasping for breath, as Talon rematerialized behind him, looking angry.

"You pathetic half-breed," Talon spat. "Do you seriously believe that you could ever defeat me? Suran was a fool to pass his gift on to you. How could an unenlightened ape like you ever hope to defeat a warrior of the Illuminate?"

"Oi! Big mouth," Mag yelled from behind him, "you dropped something."

Talon whirled around in time to see Mag throw something to Sam. The blue disc spun through the air and Sam caught it in his outstretched hand. He concentrated for an instant and his hand and the disc disintegrated into a swirling gold and blue sphere that shot across the space between him and Talon too quickly for the Illuminate warrior to dodge. The glowing ball struck his chest and Talon gasped as he once more exploded into a boiling cloud; but this time something was different. The cloud moved chaotically, horrific half-formed limbs and organs forming within it and then vanishing again in the blink of an eye. The cloud sank to the floor, where it writhed and thrashed as it slowly became solid. The pitiful thing that lay squirming on the floor in front of Sam turned his stomach. Part Illuminate, part Vore, even part human, it was a thing of nightmares.

"What . . . have . . . you . . . done . . . to . . . me?" Talon said, the twisted voice coming from the lipless, ragged hole of his mouth barely comprehensible.

"No more than you deserve," Sam said as he looked down at the revolting heap of twisted flesh in front of him.

"You . . . will . . . die . . . screaming . . . human," Talon said, his voice weakening. "You . . . will . . . all . . ."

Jay brought the foot of his Grendel down on Talon with a crunch.

"You talk too much," Jay said. A moment later the Grendel's chest popped open and Jay half slid and half fell from inside. He climbed to his feet, retching and coughing, clearing the gel from his lungs.

Sam stepped forward and hugged his friend. "Thought you were dead," he said.

"So did I," Jay said with a smile, looking up at the

immobile Grendel behind him. "These things are tougher than they look."

Doctor Stirling's voice suddenly crackled from somewhere inside the Grendel.

"I don't know if anyone can hear this, but there are three Voidborn Motherships less than forty miles away from the city and closing. If we're going to leave, we need to leave now."

Sam reached out and touched the Grendel's armored skin.

"We read you, Doctor Stirling," he said, interfacing effortlessly with the creature's systems. "We'll be with you in five minutes."

The three of them headed out of the plaza beneath the Skytree and hurried down to the drop-ship sitting on the road outside.

"Hey," Jay said as they approached the boarding ramp, "where's Rachel?"

"Get onboard," Sam said, a sudden empty feeling in the pit of his stomach. "There's something I need to tell you."


Nat and Liz walked out into the compound and over to where Jack was standing with his arm in a sling watching Will and Anne digging Adam's grave. It had been nearly forty-eight hours since the Mothership had left and there was still no sign of its return. The fallen Grendel lay in the middle of the compound, a constant reminder of their recent loss.

"Let me help," Nat said, taking the shovel from Anne and helping her up out of the hole.

"Thanks," Anne said, her face red with the exertion of digging up the frozen ground. "I'm going to go get a drink. Anyone want anything?"

"Yeah, some water would be good," Will said, stopping for a moment to rest.

"No problem," Anne said, "back in a minute."

"Here," Liz said, offering Will her hand, "my turn."

"No, it's okay," Will said. "I'm all right for a few m—"

He stopped and cocked his head to one side as he heard a strange, barely audible throbbing noise. He looked over Nat's shoulder and his mouth dropped open in surprise. The others turned and looked in the same direction, and saw the distant outline of not one but two Motherships dropping down through the clouds and heading for the city. As the Motherships drew closer over the following minutes, they could all see the clear signs of battle damage on both of the giant vessels. They looked as if they'd been to hell and back.

"Do you think they're friendly?" Will asked as they drifted ever closer.

"Maybe we'd better take cover until we know one way or the other," Liz said.

Liz helped Will up out of the hole and they all hurried

toward the dormitory block, crawling under the raised structure and hiding in the shadowy space beneath. They lay in silence for what seemed like an hour, but which was probably actually no more than a few minutes, before they heard the familiar sound of a drop-ship's engines approaching. A minute later the black triangular aircraft touched down in the compound next to the fallen Grendel, and the hatch in its side hissed open. Doctor Stirling was the first to exit the drop-ship, closely followed by a girl with strange marks on her face. They crawled out from under the dormitory and walked toward Stirling and the girl.

"Are we glad to see you guys!" Nat said happily as they approached.

Doctor Stirling didn't say anything. He just looked back at the hatch in the side of the drop-ship as Jay and Sam walked out carrying between them what was unmistakably a body wrapped in a plain, white sheet.

# 13

Sam looked down at the grave. The simple wooden cross at its head bore the single word "Rachel." Next to it was another cross that marked Adam's resting place. Sam took a deep breath and closed his eyes. He had lost so much over the past two years. He had hoped that at some point he might get used to the grief, but now he was beginning to wonder if he ever would.

"Liz said you were out here," Jay said as he walked up and stood beside his friend.

"I miss her so much," Sam said. "I keep asking myself, why couldn't it have been me?"

"I know what you mean." Jay looked at the ground. "I keep wondering if I'd made it to the top of the tower and if I'd been there when you confronted Talon, maybe . . . I dunno . . . maybe things would have turned out differently."

"We were stupid," Sam said, shaking his head, "thinking we could take Talon on like that. He was a trained soldier, a veteran of God knows how many battles. We never stood a chance. I should never have tried something so risky."

"Hey," Jay said, looking Sam straight in the eye, "it's human nature, man. You want to kid yourself that there might have been something you could have done, some way you could have fixed the roll of the dice, but that's all crap." He turned back to Rachel's grave. "And you know she would have told you exactly the same thing."

"You're right," Sam said. "Still can't help but feel that I led her to her death, though."

"So you led us," Jay said with a shrug, "that's what you do. We all had a say in the matter. Any one of us could have said no at any point, but we didn't. You know why? Because we trust you and nothing that's happened is going to change that. I get it, man. Being the leader in a situation like this sucks, but someone's got to do it. And right now that someone's you. If it hadn't been for you, Rachel, and your dad, the body count could have been ten figures, Sam. Don't ever forget that."

Sam looked down at Rachel's grave. "Price was still too high," he said, his head suddenly full of all the things that he had wanted to say to her, but now never could.

"Yeah, I know. Come on inside," Jay said. "It's too cold to be mooching around out here."

"Yeah, okay, just give me a minute," Sam said. Jay looked at him for a moment and then nodded before walking off toward the dormitory block.

Sam looked down at the two graves again and thought of everyone they'd lost: Tim, Toby, Jackson, Kate, Adam, his father, and Rachel. Too many good people.

"I'm sorry," Sam said quietly as he knelt down and placed his hand on the loose soil on top of Rachel's grave. He stayed like that for a moment and then got to his feet, turned, and walked away.

"So you have no idea what triggered your transformation," Stirling said as he shone the ophthalmoscope into each of Sam's eyes in turn.

"No idea," Sam replied. "I wasn't even consciously doing it. It just seemed completely natural, like I'd always been able to do it."

"Fascinating," Stirling said, placing the instrument down on the bench. "And you've not been able to do it since?"

"No," Sam said, shaking his head. "The only thing I can think is that Talon must have form-locked me in that final confrontation. If my father was still alive, maybe he could tell us more, but I haven't the faintest idea what Dad did to me."

"You have my sympathies," Stirling said. "Your father was a genius, but, more than that, he was a good man."

"I still don't know how I feel, to be honest," Sam said. "I mean, I believe what he told me, that my family wasn't just some sort of elaborate cover to mask his true identity, but that doesn't change the fact that he spent years lying to all of us."

"In his defense, he didn't really have a choice," Stirling said. "Shirt up, please."

"I suppose," Sam said, lifting up his T-shirt as Stirling pressed the cold metal of the stethoscope to his chest. "God only knows what I'm going to tell my mom and my sister, if we ever find them."

"When," Stirling said, "not if. And if you want my opinion you shouldn't tell them anything when that time comes. Sometimes secrets are best kept."

"You should know," Sam said with a crooked smile.

"I have kept my share in my time," Stirling said. "Well, as far as I can tell, you're perfectly healthy. The only thing that's unusual is your arm, but you knew that."

Sam held his arm up in front of him and it morphed from its golden form to looking like a perfectly normal flesh-and-blood arm.

"Little trick my dad taught me," Sam said. "Helps cut down on the weird factor."

"Your injury is nothing to be ashamed of," Stirling said, "and neither is your heritage. I believe that at the moment of his death your father transferred *something* to you. I can't be sure what it was, but I knew Daniel better than most and I know that he rarely did anything without a good reason."

"You mean Suran," Sam said, raising an eyebrow.

"Suran, Daniel Shaw, Andrew Riley, truly, what does it matter?"

"I suppose," Sam said. "Think I'll just go with Dad."

"Very wise," Stirling said with a smile.

"What have you done with Talon's men?" Sam asked. They had found Talon's human soldiers unconscious on board the Mothership after their commander's death. They had proven just as impossible to awaken as any of the rest of the planet's sleeping population.

"I had them moved to the Sleeper dormitory," Stirling replied. "I don't believe we have anything to fear from them now that Talon is dead. Their implants are still active, but without him issuing any commands I suspect that they are now no different from any other Sleeper. Don't worry, I shall be keeping a close eye on them."

"Good," Sam replied. "If you don't need me anymore, I'm going to go and sleep for a week."

"I may have some further tests to carry out," Stirling said, "but they can wait for now."

"Thanks," Sam said, grabbing his jacket and walking out of the lab, heading across the darkened compound to the dormitory block.

"Hey, you," a voice said from somewhere behind him. He turned and saw Mag sitting on top of the fallen

Grendel that still lay in the middle of the compound.

"You decided if you're staying or not yet?" Sam asked as she leaped down onto the ground and walked toward him.

"Depends," Mag said. "Do you want me to?"

"Of course I do," Sam said. "We all do."

"Think I still make some of the others a little nervous," Mag said with a wry smile.

"You worry too much," Sam said. "Besides which, we don't know how safe it is up in Scotland anymore. The Vore are still up there and they're still spreading. Stirling has some ideas about how we can slow them down, but you would be better off here."

"Don't worry," Mag said, walking alongside him toward the dormitory block. "I'm not going anywhere. This place is even starting to feel a bit like home."

"Funny, isn't it?" Sam said. "But I know exactly what you mean."

"I'm going to go and get something to eat," Mag said as they approached the entrance to the block. "You coming?"

"Nah, I'm just going to bed. I've not been sleeping brilliantly since . . . well . . . since everything," Sam said.

"Fair enough," Mag replied. "I'll see you in the morning. Jay's said he's going to teach me how to shoot properly."

"Sounds good," Sam said with a tired smile. "See you later."

He walked inside and made his way to his room. He was

just about to step inside when Nat came around the corner at the far end of the corridor.

"Hey! Sam! Hold on a sec," she shouted, jogging toward him. "I've got something for you."

She reached into her pocket and handed him a sealed envelope.

"Adam went and got it," she said as he took the envelope. "He was going to give it to you on your birthday, but, well, I figured you might want it now. You look like you could use a little cheering up."

"We all could," Sam said with a sigh. He tore open the envelope and pulled out the photograph inside. It was a picture of him with his mom, dad, and sister, that had once sat on the sideboard in the living room of their old house.

"You remember when he was asking everyone their old addresses and making jokes about what we must all have been like before the invasion . . . well, he might have had an ulterior motive."

"Thanks," Sam said, looking at the photo with a sad smile. "Really, this means a lot."

"You okay?" Nat asked, seeing the haunted look in his eyes.

"No," Sam replied, "but I will be."

Nat gave him a quick hug and then walked away as Sam stepped into his room. He locked the door behind him and went over to the old battered mirror that hung on the wall. He slid the photo of his family under the edge of the frame, just beneath the Polaroid photo of him, Jay, and Rachel standing in front of the Grendel that had once patrolled the compound outside. All three of them were making stupid faces at the camera and laughing. He let out a long sigh and stared at his tired-looking face in the mirror. A moment later his face began to shift subtly, his skin growing paler as glowing blue lines spread from the corners of his eyes back over the crested ridges of his skull.

"That's going to take some getting used to," he said, looking at the half-human, half-Illuminate face that stared back at him. He had lied to Stirling earlier; the truth was that he'd been concealing his true appearance since the final battle with Talon. He told himself that it was because he didn't want anyone to worry about him, but the reality was that he didn't want to tell them. He had no idea what change Suran had caused in him in his dying moments and now there was no one alive who could give him any real answers.

"What did you do to me, Dad?" Sam said, reaching out and touching the photo of a grinning Andrew Riley. "What did you do?"

The Voidborn stood, its head bowed in front of the black cloud that swirled endlessly in front of it.

"Were the Illuminate destroyed?" a voice from within the cloud said.

"Yes, my master," the Voidborn replied. "Though the child of the Illuminate still lives."

"For now," the voice said.

"Do you wish us to attack the captured vessels?" the Voidborn asked.

"No, that pleasure shall be mine," the voice replied. "Have the rest of our forces prepare for my arrival."

"Is there any message you would like me to pass on to them, my master?"

"Only that the final hour is at hand," the voice replied. "My journey nears its end. Their Primarch comes."